Cwall ♡

IF GIVEN A SECOND CHANCE,
WOULD YOU TAKE IT?

Given the Chance

E. L. WALL

Cover Design by Books and Moods
Editing by My Brother's Editor

CONTENT WARNING

Readers, please be advised this book is intended for readers 18+.
This novel contains explicit sexual content.

PLAYLIST

Wasted On You – Morgan Wallen

Constellations – Jack Johnson

drivers license – Olivia Rodrigo

Heart Like a Truck – Lainey Wilson

Look After You – The Fray

At Last – Etta James

Good 4 U – Olivia Rodrigo

If You Ever Did Believe – Stevie Nicks

R U Mine? – Arctic Monkeys

Heartbeat – The Fray

broken – Jonah Kagen

Us – James Bay

I Found – Amber Run

Your Song Saved My Life – U2

PROLOGUE

I guess you could say there are a few things that ultimately led to our unraveling. Or rather, our "we never really would have happened anyway." But standing in front of him now makes me question every decision I made when we were kids. What if I had said yes to that dance in seventh grade instead of going with a girlfriend who didn't have a date? What if I had the guts to just tell him how I really felt instead of being afraid of rejection? I could have gone after him when he walked away, demanding answers. Maybe it all would have been for nothing, and maybe it wouldn't have worked out anyway. But I can tell you for certain, I won't let this second chance slip by.

1

Now

I am walking down Lydon Street like I always do on Sunday mornings. I walk past the floral shop that sells the most beautiful roses you've ever seen and undoubtedly handles every Valentine's Day bouquet within ten miles of this town. A few more blocks, and I reach the coffee shop I frequent on a regular basis. Stepping inside, the bell above the door dings indicating a customer. Jules, the best barista in town and who knows my order to a T, hustles over to get it started.

"Iced caramel latte with no sugar and a blueberry scone coming right up, Eden!" she yells over the bustling customers and chatter filling the small space.

I smile and send her a quick thank you before settling in at a table by the window. Since I've come here basically every day over the last year, they've let me start a tab so I don't have to wait in line to pay each time. One of the perks of ordering the same thing every day I suppose. I wonder what they would do if I came in and suddenly ordered something random. Even if I didn't like what I ordered, I think the look on Jules's face would be reward enough.

I wouldn't say I'm necessarily a creature of habit by any means, but when I like something, I stick to it until I can no longer stomach the taste or sound. Like when it comes to music—I have always been the type to find a song I really love, listen to it a hundred times on repeat, then can't ever hear it again because I'm sick of it. I still do it every time even though I know this about myself. Just last week I probably listened to Morgan Wallen's "Wasted On You" at least fifty times.

After fifteen minutes of perusing YouTube videos, I hunker down and focus on my work. I started writing as a kid just for fun, and I am fortunate enough to have made a career out of it. I guess my mom's influence may have had something to do with it, seeing as how she's worked at a university most of my life. While most kids were enjoying summer camps around the state, I spent my summer days reading in the university's libraries and making up my own stories. It was inevitable I would go into writing as a result. I could have followed in my father's footsteps and become a musician, but I have zero music abilities and would much rather be the person dancing in the crowd than up on the stage performing.

Just then Jules arrives with my order. "Whatcha working on this week, E?" she asks as she plops down a piping hot scone and my latte, topped off with extra caramel.

"Honestly, I don't even know," I say, exasperated. "I've been sitting here in my own head too busy being distracted by YouTube instead of searching for inspiration. Sometimes writing sucks."

"I wouldn't even know how to help, considering I was a poor excuse of an English student. I'll stick to making a decent latte." She laughs as she shrugs her shoulders.

"Hey, these lattes are more than decent. I wouldn't be here every day if you didn't make your work a piece of art." She rolls her eyes in an attempt to brush off the compliment, something we both have in common actually. She doesn't take compliments too well like me. I always find myself awkwardly smiling and then changing the subject.

"Thank you, but it does help that you never change your order. If I hadn't somewhat perfected it by now, then it would be pretty sad."

We laugh as she walks away, and I attempt to focus on my work. Half my latte is gone and only a few crumbs occupy my plate when I glance up to roll my neck and stretch my back. I sense him walk past before I even get a look at his face, and every hair on my body stands on end. There's only one person my body reacts to like that, and I haven't seen him since the bar that night nearly four years ago. He's still facing the counter, and I take the opportunity to trace my eyes down every inch of his back. My heart beats erratically in my chest anticipating the moment he will turn around. There's a moment I think for sure I am hallucinating. I've been coming to this coffee shop every day for over a year, and I haven't run into him once.

A thousand memories flood my brain—the years we spent together as kids, the fight, and then the silence. If he even notices me, what are the chances he'll come and say hi? I'm equal parts terrified he won't and terrified he will.

Thirty seconds go by, feeling like hours while he finishes his order and turns. He's scrolling through something on his phone when his eyes slowly lift. As if he too can sense me, his gaze instantly finds mine. My heart rapidly beats in my chest so loudly nearby patrons can probably hear it, and then it feels as if it stops completely.

"Hi," he says as he slowly raises his arm to wave. Clearly, he thinks I'm as much of a mirage as I think he is. "Hi," I manage to choke out. Quickly realizing that sounded strangled, I speak again.I ask, thinking there's no way he remembers or even cares.

"Four years," he says matter of factly. "It's been four years, and yet I feel like I just saw you."

"I know the feeling." I laugh. "How have you been? Would you like to sit down?" My hands sit awkwardly on the table since I have no idea what else to do with them. He smiles at me like he knows how nervous I am. Noah Rivers is one of the few people who has ever been able to see through the façade I wear to keep most people at bay. I'm not great at expressing my feelings on the fly, and even though I try to mask my facial expressions to be hard read, he's always seen through it.

"I wish I could, but I'm heading to work right now. My schedule changes often, though, so maybe we can catch up another day? If you want to, of course?" He adds that last part quickly and like a question when he sees my face fall ever so slightly.

"Of course. I would love to if you're sure you have the time." *Why do I sound like a thirteen-year-old about to be kissed for the first time? Find your normal speaking voice, Eden. Christ!* "What days are you free?" I ask him as I began to open my calendar.

"I'll have to check. It's an on and off schedule based on what the other officers' shifts are. I'm not the highest rank yet, so I take what's given to me." He smiles sheepishly, and it's in that moment what he just said registers in my head and surely on my face.

"No shit. You became a cop, didn't you? Just like you always said you would when we were kids."

I can't help but beam at him now. Ever since we were ten, Noah has gone on and on about becoming a police officer, and here he is living out that dream.

"Ha, yeah. I guess I'm predictable, huh? I graduated from the academy about six months after we ran into each other."

"I can't believe you're a cop. That's amazing, Noah, really! If anyone is truly fit for it, it's you." I smile and let the quiet moment stretch for several more seconds before Noah speaks up. "Thank you, Eden, that means a lot. How about we exchange numbers, and we can try to get together this week?"

"Perfect."

He hands over his phone, and I start typing in my contact information.

"I'll text myself, so I'll have yours, too."

As I hand over his phone. our fingers graze, and I swear I felt it in my toes. Noah lingers before he stuffs his phone back into his jeans.

He smiles and starts to back away before saying, "I'll see you soon, Eden."

Those five words gave me hope that maybe second chances are more than just a fairy tale. "See you soon, Noah."

2

AGE 10

"**E**den!" An unmistakable voice rings out through the neighborhood as I ride my little Huffy bike down the slightly sloped road. "Eden, wait up!" I skid to a stop and look over my shoulder to see Noah Rivers peddling like his life depends on it to catch up to me. "Geez, when did you get so fast on that thing? Last summer you could barely sit on it." He huffs out a breath like he's actually winded, and I turn all the way around to meet him next to his bike. "Noah, why do you sound like you've never ridden a bike before? You're totally out of breath!" I laugh at him, and he nudges my shoulder to brush off the insult.

"I know how to ride my bike, Eden. But I was running around the yard with Syren when I saw you ride by so I was already out of breath!" He takes a deep lungful of air with his hands perched on his hips before peeking at me through his shaggy brown hair. "Anyway! Want to race down Lydon Street?!"

"That's the main road, Noah. You know we aren't supposed to do that. Besides, I was going to explore the woods again today, maybe see if I can find something cool. Want to come?"

He brings his hand up to his chin as if he needed to give the idea some thought. "Yeah, let's go!"

I roll my eyes at him because if there's one thing Noah is not good at, it's being mysterious. We've been friends ever since I can remember and having him live only a few houses down has ensured our friendship will be forever. We even have a handshake and promise to always be each other's best friend. I mean, I have my girl friends at school just like he has his pack of boys. But everyone kind of knows we're a package deal—wherever one goes, the other is sure to follow. We're inevitable that way.

"Let's bring Syren. He has the sniffing skills of a trained police dog. Maybe he can lead us in the direction of finding something cool since your dad won't let us use the metal detector anymore." We borrowed it once without permission and ended up breaking it. His dad had to pay a hefty price to replace the part we broke off, and it has since been put under more lockdown than a criminal.

Noah glances over at me in warning, and I know it's still a touchy topic. He got grounded forever because of our little accident. We ride our bikes back down the road until we get to his house, and he whistles for Syren. It wasn't surprising in the least when they got the dog and named him Syren. Noah has always been obsessed with police officers and claims one day he's going to be one. I personally think it would be terrifying to be a cop, but nothing bad ever really happens around here, so I guess he'll be okay.

I'm only ten years old, and I have no idea what I want to be when I grow up. The only thing I'm kind of good at is writing stories. Noah hates English class, but I'm one of the few kids who enjoys creating characters and making up stories. Mom says I have a knack for it since I've spent so much of my childhood at the university with her. She's been working there since before I was born, and that's how she met Dad. He was just out of college, pursuing a career in music, when Mom walked by, and he dropped his guitar.

I've always loved that story because it makes me feel like Dad knew she was the one for him that very first moment. I told Noah about it, and he just thought the idea of love was gross. Boys.

Mom says I'm still too young to understand the feeling of love outside of family members, but that one day I'll just know. She always said she felt instantly comfortable with Dad and that there was a spark between them. Whatever that means. I feel comfortable with Noah, but that's because he's my best friend. I could never look at him, or any other boy for that matter, any other way. So, for now, I'll stick to exploring the woods behind our houses looking for buried treasure. There's got to be something out here...I hope.

3

Now

My mind is still reeling as I gather my stuff and walk back down Lydon toward my apartment. When I woke up this morning, I never even for a second considered I might run into Noah Rivers of all people. My skin still feels hot at the memory of his fingers grazing mine when I returned his phone. God, what is wrong with me? I should not be having that reaction to him after all that's happened and after all these years.

Seeing him brought back a rush of emotions, one of which being the falling out we had had all those years ago. I shake the memory from my mind and try to focus on the present. I can't be feeling this way about him, and I can't just meet him to catch up. I was so shocked to see him in the first place that all other thoughts slipped my mind. All other thoughts including my current boyfriend. That's it, I am a terrible person.

I'm in a happy relationship, and one interaction with Noah has me catapulting into the past. I mean, what would James even say if I told him about my run-in? Sure, we had the 'ex' talk when we first got together, but Noah isn't really an ex since we never really dated. To be honest, I don't even know what to call him. My inner voice reminds me start with when you see Noah again. I gotta go, love you."

I set the phone down in my lap with the black screen facing upward at an angle just right to catch the tree line spread out across the pond's edge.

"You're probably right," I whisper to myself as I glance up to see the water rippling from a fallen leaf.

4

AGE 12

I hang the sparkly red dress back on the rack and glance to my left. Chloe is a few feet away, making a weird face at a puke-green-colored dress. "Who on earth designed this and thought the color choice was a good idea?"

With one more disgusted look, she hangs it back on the rack next to a zebra print dress with a pink sash across it. I walk over to a rack of black dresses, ignoring the voice in my head telling me to try more color. Ever since starting middle school, I've gravitated toward black. Not because I'm trying to be goth or emo, but because Mom always says black is a slimming color on every woman. At the age of twelve, I already had a few insecurities, and if wearing black works for Mom and makes her feel good, then I hoped it would do the same for me.

"E, are you really going to go with black *again*?" Chloe tilts her head at me with a tsk, expecting me to put it back and try on the lime green one in her outstretched hand instead.

"First of all, I like black, and second of all, that dress is hideous, so you should put it right back where you found it." I laugh and turn my attention back to the black dresses lined up along the rack across from her.

Chloe peers at me through thick lashes caked in mascara as she places the lime green monstrosity back on the rack. She started wearing makeup when we started sixth grade and has since mastered her look. I tried wearing eyeliner for our sixth-grade school pictures and ended up looking like a raccoon who didn't know how to smile. I've taken a makeup hiatus since then.

I find a really simple black dress with delicate spaghetti straps lined with little fake crystals and slowly pull it off the rack to get a better look. With no warning, Chloe comes up behind me and sighs loudly enough for other customers to look at us. I jump and slap her on the arm quickly before turning back to the dress.

"I know it's black, but I really like the simplicity of it—"

Before I can finish my thought, she cuts in and says, "The straps *are* really pretty...fine! Try it on because it'll probably be perfect, but next dance, you are trying on some color, Eden. I'm serious!" She fixes me with a stern look, the one like my mom gives me when she wants me to do something.

"Deal," I reply, knowing that by the next dance, I'll come up with some excuse to wear black again.

After getting home from dress shopping that afternoon, I see Noah heading over through my front yard.

"Hey! Find a dress for the dance?" he asks, taking a seat on the front steps as I walk over with my bags in hand.

"Yeah, I found a really simple dress that I like, it's—"

But before I can finish, Noah cuts in and says, "Black. I figured, Eden, you're very predictable, you know?"

With a scoff, I dig in and tell him that he's one to talk, considering he's the predictable one. Last week during career day at school, one of the teachers asked him what he wanted to do after college, and before he could respond, his best friend Ryder piped up for him and said, "Oh come on, everyone knows Noah wants to be a cop!"

He laughs at the memory before his face becomes more serious as he looks down at his hands. "Well, how's this for predictable? Want to go with me to the dance on Friday?" He's still looking down at his hands when I respond awkwardly.

"Yeah, I thought we were all going together. Lane, Ryder, Chloe, and Gabe, right?"

Noah lifts his head and nods. Sounds good. We'll all go as a group." When he stands up, he starts to back away down the front walk. "I gotta start my homework. I'll see you tomorrow."

Before I can even say okay, he's jogging up the street toward his house. I could be totally wrong here, but did he want me to go with him as, like, his date?!

"Chloe, I know I just saw you, but when you get this message, call me."

I toss the phone on my bed and pace my bedroom. I stop in the middle of the room, hands on my hips when I hear a knock at my door. "Come in."

"Hey, did you pick a dress at the mall with Chloe?" my older sister, Callie, asks as she shuffles into the room with a bowl of popcorn in hand.

"Uh, yeah. It's hanging over there by my closet. It's black," I say with a shrug, waiting for the inevitable comment to follow.

Callie gets up, abandoning her bowl of popcorn on my bed to sneak a peek at my dress inside the garment bag. "Wow. I love it, E. Good choice. You should wear those long crystal earrings with it. They'll match the straps." She takes her spot on my bed again and plucks a handful of popcorn from the bowl.

"But it's black. Aren't you going to lecture me about choosing more color instead of always going the safe route?"

"Why?" she asks. "I'm not the one wearing it. You are. You wouldn't have bought it if you didn't like it or feel good in it, right?"

"Right," I say.

"Then there you go. You shouldn't pick something someone else likes because that's what they want you to wear. Pick what you like, and if that means black, then that's cool."

I stare at her, waiting for her to laugh or make a snide comment about how gullible I am, but she doesn't. She just reaches into the bowl and grabs another handful of popcorn. Callie is three years older than me. She's a sophomore in high school now, so most days I feel like I'm just the annoying little sister who embarrasses her. But I don't know. Maybe we've reached a turning point where we can get along. God, Mom would probably cry if she saw this moment.

I take advantage of this opportunity and ask Callie a question I never thought I would.

"Cal, I know it's super lame and all, but would you maybe help me get ready for the dance on Friday?"

I start twisting my fingers through the loops of my comforter waiting for her to tell me no, something she would have easily done just a year ago. Instead, she stands with her bowl of popcorn and heads for my bedroom door.

"I'd be happy to, Eden. You know, I know we've had our fair share of fights as sisters and all, but I am here for you. You can always ask me for help. I won't bite your head off."

I chuckle at the memory of her legitimately trying to bite my head when I was a baby and she was three because she was mad that Mom and Dad had me. Of course, I have no memory of the actual event, but it's one of Dad's favorite stories to tell at holiday get-togethers.

"Thanks, Callie, I appreciate it. But don't tell Mom we're getting along yet. She'll probably cry or something and expect us to be best friends."

She nods her head in agreement. "Oh, don't worry. We'll find better ways to mess with her." She winks and slips past the door, shutting it quietly behind her.

Great, I have a dress I like, and my sister has agreed to help me with my makeup so I don't go to the dance looking like a raccoon. The only problem now is trying to figure out why going to the dance as a group somehow upset Noah. We're just friends, aren't we? I lay back on my bed and fiddle with the comforter again, a nervous habit. I shoot out of bed and send off a quick AIM to Noah since he's online. **You're cool with us all going as a group Friday, right?**

The little typing bubble pops up, disappears, then reappears again before his response lights up the screen. **Totally cool.**

So, why do I get the feeling it's not cool at all?

5

NOW

It's been three days since I ran into Noah, and I haven't heard anything from him. He said he would reach out once he knew his schedule for the week, but he hasn't. I know I'm being silly and acting like a schoolgirl, but I don't want to be the one to text him first. The thought occurs to me that maybe he feels the same way.

I roll out of bed and head toward the bathroom to take a shower when my phone buzzes with an incoming text. I race back to my bed to retrieve it when I trip over the rug, grab the bed to stabilize myself. and land in a heap in a pile of blankets. Mom always said I had an obsession with soft blankets, and clearly the obsession has carried over to adulthood. Pulling the blankets off my head, I rifle through them in search of my phone. When I finally grab it, I unlock it in hopes of seeing a text from Noah, but I see James's name instead.

My shoulders slump in disappointment, and I instantly feel guilt. Since when do I get bummed about a text from my boyfriend? That's right, my boyfriend of two years who is nothing but sweet and respectful. Who holds the door open for me at restaurants, who remembers my favorite candy, and always comes over with a Twix bar. James, the man who literally drove to CVS to pick up a box of tampons for me last month when I got my period and ran out. I push aside my disappointment because again, that's awful, and open the text.

James: Hey, babe. Sorry I missed you this past weekend 😔 **Let's have date night tomorrow to make up for it?**

I read it again three times before getting up to take my shower. I'll respond to him later.

I let the hot water cascade down my back before pooling at the base of the tub. I stare down at the swirling tornado of water rushing down the drain, and water drips over my face. I lean against the cool tiles, relishing the cold feel against my back in contrast to the scalding water at my front. I've always been a hot shower taker; I like the water so hot my skin is usually beet red by the time I get out.

As the water trails down my chest in between my breasts, I get lost in my thoughts. Suddenly I'm not alone in the shower. I feel strong warm hands wrap around my waist and tug me against chiseled abs. Before I can let out a gasp of surprise, one hand comes up to my mouth and lightly covers it while the other hand slowly ascends to my right breast. I close my eyes and allow myself to give into the feeling. As his warm hand starts kneading my breast, the other hand lowers from my mouth and slowly trails down the side of my neck. My breath hitches, and he reaches around and grasps all my hair in a firm hold and tugs so that I'm forced to look at him. My eyes flutter open to find Noah standing behind me with some impressive length pressing into my backside.

Before I even have a chance to process how this is happening, a loud bang pulls me from my reverie. My eyes snap open, and my surroundings come into focus. Quickly I turn off the shower and wrap myself in a towel before bustling to the front door.

"Who is it?" I manage to choke out in a breathy tone.

"It's Chloe! I've been calling you!" she yells from the other side of the door. "Let me in, you freak. I have questions."

I open the door to see her standing there with an umbrella and two lattes.

"Before you ask, it's your favorite since you never try anything else, and Jules knows what you like. I didn't even have a chance to order you something new before she started making it." She hands over the cup and rolls her eyes as she shakes off the rain and sets down her jacket. "It's been three days, and you haven't filled me in on the happenings with Noah. What gives?" Chloe plops into one of the armchairs across from the kitchen island and takes a bite out of her bagel.

"Clearly there is nothing to tell if you haven't heard from me. I called you minutes after I ran into the guy; don't you think if there was more to tell I would have, oh I don't know, told you?" I yell, even though I'm not actually angry with her.

"Damn, Godzilla, don't get sassy with me. He hasn't reached out yet, I take it."

He hasn't. And whatever. It's not like I was expecting him to call me the second he got his schedule to set something up," I say as I take the seat opposite her with an obvious thump.

She eyes me over her coffee cup, and instantly I know that look.

"What? Just say what's on your mind, Chlo. We both know you will eventually. So, spit it out."

She lifts her shoulders then releases them as she looks up at me sheepishly. "I mean, isn't that what you were expecting?" She puts both hands up when I start to protest. "Sorry, sorry. Wrong choice of words there. Isn't that what you were hoping for at least?"

I mull it over for a minute before shrugging and standing to make my way to my room. If we're going to talk about this, I'm not going to do it in my towel after having a shower where I fantasized about Noah touching me. We aren't not done with this conversation, missy."

"Chill, I'm getting dressed because as you can see, I just got out of the shower." I motion down my body clad in a towel still.

"Whatever, it's not like we haven't had conversations like this in all states of dress," she says flatly. "What were you doing in there anyway? I must have knocked on your door thirty times before you answered. Your neighbors even peaked out a few times to give me a death stare." She throws herself onto my bed and picks up last month's edition of Cosmo, and starts aimlessly flipping through the articles.

"I was showering. Usually when one showers, they have water cascading over them and are too busy relaxing to pay attention to outside noises." I pull on a pair of distressed jeans and a white tank top before grabbing my brush.

As I'm combing through my hair, my mind travels back to that fantasy again. I know it's wrong to fantasize about another man when you're clearly in a relationship, but Mom always said looking is okay if you don't touch. That applies here, too, right? Too deep in thought I miss the pillow hurtling toward my head and thwacking me before falling limp to the floor.

"Earth to Eden! Geez, what were you just so engrossed in that you didn't hear me talking to you? I haven't had to throw a pillow at you like that since like ninth grade."

"I—nothing, I was just thinking." I rub the spot where the pillow hit me and continue brushing my hair.

"You do know I know you better than anyone, right? We just went over this the other day. You were thinking about Noah just now, correct?"

I nod my head without looking at her.

"Okay, I can figure this out. It doesn't take a rocket scientist." She shuffles into a seated position with one hand in her lap, the other caressing her chin in that way people do when they're trying to look deep in thought.

"I show up here and have to knock on the door MANY times before you answer me in a towel fresh from the shower. Your face was all flushed and dewy, and then you immediately jump on me about not having heard from Noah while...holy shit! You were fantasizing about him in the shower, weren't you?!" She jumps from the bed as she shrieks her last statement. "You were totally imagining him in there with you!"

I take a few steps backward and try to escape to the kitchen to avoid continuing this conversation, but before I can make out of my bedroom door, Chloe's arm snakes out and grabs me in a death grip.

"Whoa, watch the claws there, miss mani-pedi. I have no idea what you're talking about!" I pull my arm from her grip and head back to the counter to retrieve my abandoned latte. As I take a much-needed sip, she leans on the counter with a bored expression on her face. "E, we both know that's a lie, and I'm honestly offended you thought you could get away with it."

"What do you want me to say, Chloe? I feel terrible about this whole situation, and nothing has even happened yet!" I huff, then shuffle over to the couch and face plant onto it. "Am I a bad person? Tell me the truth," I mumble into the cushions.

"I already told you my thoughts on the matter, Eden. You need to be honest with yourself and honest with James. It's that simple."

"Ugh, again with the whole being right thing. It's annoying. Are we still having our girl's night tomorrow? I look forward to our Thursday wine nights, and it's been a few weeks since we've all been able to meet up."

She puts her jacket back on and grabs her umbrella, indicating her lunch break is nearing its end and she has to head back to work.

"It's still on. Stella is hosting this week and has a cheese plate covered. Didn't you read the group chat message?" she asks as she heads for the door.

To be honest, I've been so wrapped up in this Noah thing that I hadn't even looked at my text messages, including the three unread ones from James. "Yes, I saw it, just spaced it. I'll see you tomorrow. Thanks for the pick-me-up." I lift my latte in salute as she opens the door.

"Think about what I said, E, and be prepared to talk about it *a lot* tomorrow when we get together. You know Stella and Emmy are going to want details."

"Yeah, yeah." I wave her off and sink back into the couch once she leaves.

How am I supposed to focus on work or anything else for that matter? I glance over at my phone while biting my lip.

"Maybe I *can* be the one to text first?" I mumble to myself as I rotate the phone clockwise in my hands.

With a sigh, I quickly unlock my phone and shoot off a quick text before I lose my nerve. My finger hovers over the send button before slamming it down, then tossing my phone across the couch.

"Shit."

8

AGE 12

I didn't see Noah all weekend, and when I went by his house, his mom said he wasn't feeling well. I tried instant messaging him, but he was off-line, too. Maybe he really was sick, and that's why he left the dance so abruptly. *Or maybe you really hurt his feelings by turning down his dance, Eden.*

"Shut up!" I say as I whack the side of my head. My inner monologue can be such a bitch sometimes. I'm not allowed to use words like that because Mom would ground me, but when it's to myself and only in my head, then it doesn't count. I'm not dumb. I know it's because he's mad at me. But if he would just give me five minutes to explain, then we could move past this.

I don't want him to think I rejected him, even though that's exactly what it looked like. I've never really given too much thought to whether I like Noah as more than a friend. I just always assumed there's no way he could ever see me like that, so I thought the same. But now that we haven't spoken in a few days, I'm starting to worry there is more than friendship there. What if he doesn't forgive me, and we can't move past this? I don't even realize I'm pacing my room until I bump my hip into the side of my desk. "Ow! You bitch!" I'm rubbing the side of my hip already knowing there will be a bruise there place tomorrow when there's a quick, sharp knock at my door. My mom enters before I say anything,

"Eden Elizabeth, did you just curse?" She stands there with her hands on her hips and a pointed stare waiting for me to answer her.

"I'm sorry. I walked into my desk and bruised my hip. It was an impulse. I won't do it again."

She can see it on my face the lack of teenage defiance she was expecting from me and lowers her arms.

"Talk about what?" I look up at her with mock confusion.

She's my mom. Moms know everything that goes on with their kids. Or at least mine does. She gives me a look that tells me she isn't buying it. I heave a sigh and sit down on the edge of my bed. "Something happened at the dance with Noah, and he hasn't talked to me since. His mom said he was sick, but I don't know. I have a feeling there's more to it."

"Do you want to tell me what happened?"

I give her the rundown of Lane being upset and Noah asking me to dance. I give her the Reader's Digest version and wait for her to give me some motherly advice.

"Sounds to me like you did the best you could in that situation, E. Maybe he really is just sick, and everything is fine. Give him a few more days and try talking to him about it—clear the air. You two have been inseparable for years. Something like this won't derail your friendship."

She pats my knee and gives me a shoulder squeeze before slipping out the door and shutting it quietly behind her. Maybe she's right. I'm overacting. We'll talk in a few days, and everything will go back to normal.

Well, it's been three weeks since Noah started avoiding me, and it's clear he's upset about the dance, and I was, in fact, not overreacting.

The bus crawls to a stop at our bus stop on the corner of our street, and Noah is off it in two seconds flat. I scramble after him and call his name. He doesn't even have the decency to turn around and look at me. He just keeps walking.

"Noah!" I yell as I speed walk after him trying not to cause a scene in front of the kids still on the bus. I jog up beside him and then step in front of him, so he has to look at me. "What is your problem? You've been avoiding me for three weeks! Is this because of what happened at the dance?"

"I don't want to talk about the dance, Eden." He keeps walking, but I grab his arm to stop him.

I say, exasperated.

"Yeah, well that's how it felt to me," he says coldly and scuffs his sneaker on the concrete.

"Hey, look at me. That's not what happened, and if you had given me five minutes to explain or waited for me to come back, then we could have avoided this whole three weeks of tension."

I wait for him to reply and say he understands or at least say *something*, but he doesn't. He just keeps scuffing his foot on the ground.

"Noah, I'm sorry I hurt your feelings. I was just trying to be there for Lane. I never thought you would be this upset. W"re friends, and we should have been able to talk this through."

"You're right, Eden. We're just friends."

With that, he turns away from me and heads for his house. I just stand there watching his retreating figure, wondering what just happened. It's not until he's completely out of sight that I realize—I may have just lost my best friend.

Months go by, and Noah and I don't speak. It's as if we were never friends to begin with. All our adventures in the woods, playing ding-dong ditch, prank calling the neighbors. All of it just erased over a simple misunderstanding.

Summer came and went, and we're officially eighth graders. I was hoping to take our traditional first day of school picture in front of the magnolia tree in front of my house like we do every year. But he never showed up. Mom took a picture of Callie and I, but I was acutely aware of my missing best friend. He stopped taking the bus to school, too. He started riding his new bike instead. His parents gave him a Trek for his birthday over the summer, and I was so excited for him. Even though I couldn't share that excitement with him, I was still happy for him. I may not be his best friend anymore, but Noah Rivers is still mine.

It's true what they say. You don't realize what you have until it's gone.

9

NOW

Stella's place is an eclectic collection of mismatched furniture and black currant candles. She has the style of an icon and owns more designer handbags than I could ever dream of. Her aunt works in New York City and often sends designer things to her not just for birthdays and holidays, but just because it's Tuesday. It sounds like a joke, but it's for real. Last year she got a Louis Vuitton handbag with a note attached saying *'Happy Tuesday, darling! Miss you!'* We were all more than a little shocked, but judging by the look on Stella's face, this wasn't the first time she'd gotten something like that.

I walk into her apartment and set down the canvas tote I brought with two bottles of wine in it and grab a slice of pepperjack cheese on my way to the fridge. I fill my glass with some ice cubes and grab the wine opener.

"Well, I see we're jumping right in tonight," Stella says from the barstool she's perched on.

Emmy walks in right then, wielding a tray of fresh brownies that immediately makes my mouth water. Brownies are one of my weaknesses, and there are few things in life that smell better than when they're fresh out of the oven. Emmy makes the best brownies, too.

They're always extra chocolatey and gooey. I predict I'll eat at least four tonight and thoroughly regret it tomorrow. Oh well, another problem for another day.

"Yes, we are. And I plan on eating half those brownies, Emmy. They smell amazing." She gives me a one-arm hug as she passes me on her way to the cupboard. She puts the tray down and grabs a glass to join us at the bar.

"Well, now that we're all here, let's get right down to business. Have you heard from him?" Chloe asks, looking directly at me as Stella and Emmy lean in waiting for a response.

I sigh and look down at my wineglass. "He texted me late last night when I was falling asleep. Took me forever to finally go to sleep after his last text." I pull out my phone and show them what he sent.

Stella lets out a low whistle and says, "Damn, I can feel the sexual tension through that text message. What the hell are you going to do when you see him?"

"I don't know," I groan into my hands. "I told James last night when he came by. He said he trusts me and that it's not a big deal to catch up with an old friend. It's not like an ex or old flame." They all look at me at the same time.

"Hey, his words, not mine," I say with both arms raised in surrender.

"Eden, we all know he isn't an ex or an old flame per se, but you two are definitely something." Chloe looks at me then down at her glass before meeting my gaze again. "Listen, we all have that one person, right? The one where we wished something could have been but never was. Mine is Blake Sanders. Remember him? Nothing will ever happen between us because he's engaged, and honestly, I'm happy for him. But of course, I'm always going to have a soft spot for him and wonder. Noah is yours. But you're being given a second chance here to figure it out. As much as I love James, you need to feel this out. You don't want to look back in twenty years and have regrets that he was the one who got away." The room falls silent as we all consider Chloe's words. Emmy breaks the silence first. "She's right, Eden. James is an amazing guy, but if he's not the one, then he's not the one."

"You owe it to yourself to try. We all know how much Noah has meant to you since you were a kid. Me especially since I saw the chemistry between the two of you," Chloe adds. "Maybe this is your second chance."

I came here tonight thinking they were all going to be Team James and say that I already have a good thing, and it's crazy to jeopardize that with temptations. But as the night goes on, and conversations ebb and flow, I keep coming back to one thing…maybe this is our second chance.

10

AGE 14

Callie and I stand in front of the magnolia tree just like we do every year on the first day of school. This is the second year now Noah isn't by my side to take our first day of school picture together. We start ninth grade today; Callie is a senior. This is the only year of high school I'll have at the same time as her, and I'm hoping since we've grown closer this past year, she'll show me the ropes a little.

"Girls, look here!" Mom holds up her phone and snaps at least twenty photos in various poses. With a smirk on her face, she turns the phone to show us the last photo, and both Callie and I burst out laughing. In the last picture, I'm sticking my tongue out at Callie while she's looking cross-eyed at the camera.

"That one is my favorite," I say.

"Agreed," Callie chimes in as she slings her backpack on her shoulder. "We should get going though." We both hug Mom and climb into Callie's used Honda Accord. Mom and Dad got it for her for her sixteenth birthday, another thing Noah wasn't around for.

"Have a great first day girls. Dad and I will be home this evening, and we'll have our traditional spaghetti and meatball dinner with homemade garlic bread." She beams as she says this because ever since we were kids, she has made the same meal for the first day of school. I'm not even sure what started it, but it's become a tradition, and we never complain. Dad makes homemade pasta sauce from my grandmother's recipe, and Mom makes killer garlic bread. My mouth is watering just at the thought, and it's only seven thirty in the morning.

When we get to school Callie wanders off with her senior friends, and I see Lane flag me down. I jog over to her so we can compare class schedules. We only have two classes together this year, which will be a huge adjustment for us, considering we've had classes together since first grade when Lane moved here. Chloe meets us by the front entrance and shows us her schedule. We both cheer when we see we have four classes together. I don't miss the face Lane makes, though, when she hears the news.

By the end of the day, I'm exhausted heading into seventh period—computers. If I had to pick a class to end the day with, though, this would be it. I heard from Callie and her friends that Mr. Verga is the best. He's laid back and has a good sense of humor. It helps that he's also one of the younger teachers at the school and ridiculously handsome. Thinking about that distracts me as I'm walking into class, so I don't notice who I sit down next to until it's too late. All the other seats in the room are taken, and I glance over to see Noah staring right at me. Considering we haven't talked much since seventh grade, I give him a weak smile and focus on my notebook in front of me.

"Hey," Noah says in a completely normal voice that makes me practically choke on the air as I inhale.

"Um, hi…Noah." I look back at my notebook and open it up to start drawing doodles as we wait for Mr. Verga to start class. The forty-five-minute class goes by fast, and when the bell rings, I startle in my seat causing Noah to chuckle.

"I see you're still jumpy." He smiles at me, and it almost feels like the fight never happened. It feels like old times again. I smile and focus on collecting my backpack. Maybe it feels like old times, but it's not, and we both know it. How can he just casually talk to me as if he hasn't been freezing me out for a year and a half? I get up and start to exit the classroom when Noah catches up to me.

"Do you want to walk home with me today?" he asks calmly and waits for me to answer him.

"You want to walk home with me?" I asked him, thinking for sure I heard him wrong. "Why?" I blurt out before I realize how rude it probably sounds. He drops his gaze to the ground and scuffs his foot against the pavement. I guess that's still a habit of his.

"You don't have to, sorry. I just…I don't know. I miss hanging out with you, Eden. I'm sorry I overreacted about the dance. It was dumb, and I kick myself over it all the time. I've wanted to reach out for a while now, but I was too embarrassed and thought maybe it didn't bother you that we aren't friends anymore. I—I'm sorry, Eden, really." He starts to walk away, but I jog after him.

"So, who did you get for English this year? I heard Mrs. Landry is strict."

He looks up at me and smiles."Of course I got her." We both laugh and fall into step with each other as we walk home. This right here is the moment I've been hoping for the last year and a half. Maybe there's more we should talk abou,t but maybe there's not. Some things don't need to be analyzed. We had a lapse for a while, but I'm still Eden, and he's still Noah. Maybe we can just go back to the way things were before.

As we round the corner onto our street, Noah hesitates for a second before turning around to face me. "I'm sorry about the magnolia tree…I know its tradition, and it killed me to miss the last two." I know the feeling because the start of eighth grade sucked without him there to carry on my mom's tradition.

"Well, it's only the first day of school, so let's take a picture tomorrow for the second day." I shrug knowing it sounds cheesy but also hoping he takes me up on it.

"Sounds perfect." He says and starts to walk backward. "Dress to impress, E!" he yells as he gets closer to his house. I wave at him and walk into my house with the first genuine smile I've worn in months.

11

Now

I'm standing in my bedroom wearing nothing but a bra and underwear as I stare into my closet. I keep thinking something new will pop up, like when you go to the fridge a second and third time hoping new food will have magically appeared since the last time you checked.

I'm trying to find an outfit for tonight, and I already know I'm overthinking it. I'm meeting Noah in thirty minutes at a pub in town, so I don't need to dress up, but I also want to look good. I shouldn't even be putting this much thought into it, but I can't help myself. When I saw him on Sunday, I was in leggings and a lightweight sweater sans makeup, so clearly, I wasn't making an impression.

But now, tonight, I want to look put together. I reach into my dresser drawer and pull out my favorite pair of dark skinny jeans with frayed bottoms and a tight black shirt. Knowing Noah, he'll probably point out I'm wearing black. Old habits die hard. I keep my hair down in loose waves and only do a soft makeup look. Foundation, a little highlighting, and some mascara. I've never been one to cake on makeup and dress up in heels to go out, so I want to stay as true to myself as possible, even as my insides are screaming at me to sex it up a bit.

"You have a boyfriend, Eden. This isn't a first date. You're catching up with an old friend, that's it," I tell myself in the mirror.

I check the time and decide I should probably walk to the pub since it's only a few blocks away. It's nice out tonight so I grab a light jacket to throw on and head out the door. Halfway down the stairs, I realize I'm still wearing flip flops and rush back up to put on my Doc Martens.

I make my way into the pub and start looking around for Noah. When I don't see him, I grab a spot near the back, a high-top table with two chairs. I shoot off a quick text to let him know I'm here and where I'm sitting. He responds immediately, *'Two minutes away, sorry!'*

As soon as I see him walk through the door and weave his way toward the table I'm sitting at in the back, my breath hitches. This is bad. I shouldn't be having this kind of reaction to him. James, Eden. Remember to mention you have a boyfriend, or this could go downhill real fast. That should be my focus right now, but I can't even breathe as he draws closer, and I catch the scent of his cologne washing over me. I stand to give him a hug just as he reaches the table.

"I'm so happy we're doing this," he says into my hair, and he hugs me close. I smile, and we each take a seat at the table.

"What's your drink of choice?" he asks as he looks over the draft beer list.

"I usually go with a sangria," I reply as I set my menu down. A few minutes later a waitress comes by to take our drink order, and I don't miss the way she eyes Noah up and down. Once we've given her our drink order, I really start to feel my nerves.

"So, how do you like being a police officer?" I ask as I smile across the table at him, already knowing what his answer will be.

"I love it. It's exactly what I always hoped it would be. Don't get me wrong, the academy was tough, and the mental shit you have to get past was often harder than the physical stuff. But I love what I do." He smiles so big it's just how I always imagined he'd look when he got his dream job.

"What about you? I'm not surprised you're wearing black," he says with a chuckle, and I have to resist rolling my eyes because I *knew* he was going to say that. "You know what's funny. When I was getting ready, I said to myself that you would comment on me wearing black." I laugh and continue. "I guess I haven't changed that much over the years. My mom's voice is always in the back of my mind saying, '*black is a flattering color on everyone, dear.*'"

He looks at me ready to say something but stops. When we were kids, I always felt like I could read Noah's mind, almost like we had a telepathic power between the two of us. I wish I could say that's still there between us, but so much time has passed since we were kids.

The conversation flows surprisingly well throughout the night. I haven't found the right time to bring up James. There's never going to be a right moment, so I bite the bullet and blurt out a random question. "So, your girlfriend didn't mind you meeting up with an old friend tonight?" I ask hoping he'll say he has a girlfriend, while also praying he doesn't.

"Way to ask out of left field, E," he laughs but then continues."I don't have a girlfriend right now. Haven't in about a year. What about you? Your boyfriend didn't mind you meeting up with me?" He looks at me, waiting for me to give the same kind of response he just did, and I so badly wish I could say I'm single, too.

"Actually, he didn't mind. He thought it was cool thatI ran into someone from my childhood." I can't even look at him to see what kind of facial expression he's wearing right now. Instead, I twirl the cherry around in my drink by the stem before popping it off.

"What's his name?" he asks calmly as he picks up his drink. I tell him his name, about how we met, and how long we've been dating. "That's great, Eden. I'm happy for you." The words falling from his mouth are sincere, but it's the slight look in his eye that makes me think. H"s disappointed.

"I need to confess something, though." I swirl the melting ice around in my glass, take a deep breath, and try to muster some bravery to get this off my chest. "I was so shocked to run into you that it took me a day or two to wrap my mind around what it could mean. James is amazing. He's been such a great boyfriend, and I really do love him." I look down at the cherry stem in my hands, twirling it between my fingers again before continuing.

"But there's something missing. I didn't realize I'd been feeling that way until I saw you in the café on Sunday. I'm probably putting my foot in my mouth and assuming the wrong thing here, but I don't think I can walk away from tonight not knowing if I'll ever see you again…I can't do that again."

I still haven't lifted my eyes to look at him when I feel a warm hand close around mine. A warmth spreads from my hand all the way to my toes. My heart beats faster, and I slowly lift my head to look at him. He's watching our hands intertwine on the tabletop, and I can see his Adam's apple work in his throat as he tries to swallow.

"Eden, I know you have a boyfriend, and I will never do anything to compromise that or get in the way of that. But everything you just said is what's been on my mind for the last four years. The thought of walking away from you tonight and not even trying to at least be friends again kills me."

"One day at a time?" I ask him, all while I still hold his hand.

"One day at a time," he agrees.

12

AGE 14

It's early October and already the air feels crisper. Fall is my favorite season, and Halloween is my favorite holiday, both of which Noah knows. He's already asked me if I want to go trick-or-treating, or if we're too old for that. I say we're never too old to be a kid, and thankfully, he agreed.

Things have been weird around here the last few days since we found out my uncle is going to jail. He got into some things he shouldn't have, and well, it caught up to him. I was on AIM telling Noah a little about it when he said he had to eat dinner with his family, but that he'd be back soon. Lane is at a family member's house celebrating her mom's birthday, and Chloe is still at cheerleading practice.

There's no one else I really want to talk to right now, so I sit in the den spinning in the computer chair. I'm about to get up when I hear a light tap at the window. I pull the shade and find Noah standing there in a sweatshirt smiling at me. "I have to walk to the store to grab milk. Walk with me?"

I grab a jacket and meet him at the front door. We walk quietly for a few minutes before he asks if I'm okay. A part of me doesn't want to talk about it. I just want to sit by myself and think. I've always been one to walk away from stress and deal with my feelings on my own, but something about Noah makes me feel comfortable opening up.

Before heading to the convenience store, he tugs my arm, and we cross the street to the pond. He walks over to a bench and motions for me to join him. This pond has been here my whole life, but we have never really come here together. Neither one of us knows how to fish, and it's not big enough to skate on in the winter. We sit quietly for a few minutes, and neither one of us feels the need to fill the silence. That's something I love about being with Noah. I never feel pressure to come up with something to talk about. We can just sit peacefully together enjoying each other's company.

"Have you ever watched the movie *Pleasantville*?" Noah asks me out of the blue.

"I don't think so, why?"

"We should watch it. I think you'd like it," he says plainly.

"Okay, let's watch it." I say.

He stands quickly and motions to the convenience store, so I follow him. "Pick a snack." He gestures to the aisles of treats in the store.

"Wait, you want to watch it tonight?" I ask, a little surprised he meant right now.

"Sure. It's a Saturday night. Let's get some junk food and watch it together. My house or yours?" I look at him and crack a smile as I grab a Twix bar off the shelf.

He reaches for the same thing smiling at me. "Nothing better than a Twix bar. Whenever I'm feeling down, this helps," he says with a shrug.

"Let's go," I say as we walk toward the counter. "Wait, Noah, the milk!" I say quickly, and he turns around to grab it.

"Thanks, I definitely forgot."

Later that night we settle into a bed of blankets on the floor of his basement rec room and watch *Pleasantville*. During certain parts of the movie, he would glance over at me to gauge my reaction. I wasn't exactly expecting him to watch me watch the sex scene with Reese Witherspoon, but he did. I would never admit it out loud, but my body was hyperaware of the way he was looking at me, and it felt...good. At the end of the scene, Paul Walker's character is getting into his car when he notices a red rose in the bush along the driveway. I looked at Noah to ask him if he noticed that part before.

He smiles at me and says, "Yeah, I've seen this movie a dozen times, Eden." Then returns his gaze back to the TV. It could be a coincidence, but the night of the Valentine's dance, Noah brought me a single red rose. I've always loved red roses, something he was aware of, but a little part of me hopes he also had this part of the movie in the back of his mind.

My hand slides off the side of my stomach and brushes against Noah's. I'm about to apologize and pull it away when he grabs it gently and holds it in his. I don't say anything or try to pull away, and he doesn't say anything either. We just stay like that until the movie ends. It's the first time I've ever held his hand, and I don't want to let it go once the movie is over. Noah turns the TV off and turns his head toward me slowly. "I should probably head home," I blurt out, already getting to my feet. He stands with me and offers to walk me home even though it's only three houses down.

We walk slowly under the streetlights, and I tell him I really liked the movie, especially Reese Witherspoon. I think she might be my new favorite actress, not that I really had one to begin with, but still. I go to thank him for making me feel better about my uncle when he says my name. Something about the way he whispers '*Eden*' is enough to make every hair on my body stand. I can feel the goose bumps as they slowly cover my body inch by inch. I try to say yes, but it comes out as a squeak, earning me a smile from Noah. He lifts his hand toward my face and brushes my hair behind my ear. I'm pretty sure I stopped breathing as I felt his body shift toward mine. I knew what was about to happen, and yet I was still surprised when his lips softly touched mine.

He pulled back to look at me, my eyes still closed when he whispered my name again. Slowly my eyelids flutter open to meet his eyes. "Was that okay?" he asks quietly. "I should have asked you first, but I've been wanting to do that all night."

I smile and look down at my grass-stained Converse sneakers before looking back up to him. "I'm glad you did it because I wouldn't have had the guts to do it myself."

We both laugh, and he leans in waiting for me to give him the okay to do it again. I lift my face to his and weave my arms around his waist as he holds my face in both hands. I've never felt more in tune with someone than this moment right here. My first kiss. Some of my friends have already had their first kiss and think fourteen is late. But if I had rushed it with anyone else, it wouldn't have been right, and it wouldn't have been Noah.

13

NOW

Walking into my parents' house always makes me feel like I'm a kid again. The nostalgic smell of crisp apples and incense burning filters throughout the cozy, cape-style house. Mom has always loved the smell, and coincidentally, she makes an amazing apple pie. Dad has been burning incense for as long as I can remember. A part of me wonders if it reminds him of his college days studying music, that, or how much weed he used to smoke.

I round the corner and find my parents perched at the breakfast bar Mom is flipping through coupons, and Dad is reading a magazine about the Beatles. Something about their quiet stillness together brings a smile to my face. When I imagine being married and having a partner to go through life with, this is what I picture. Not expensive trips or a fancy wedding, not dinner reservations and gift giving at Christmas. But these contented moments and feeling completely at ease with the person you love most.

Dad catches me staring at them and rests his magazine on the counter. "Good morning, Eden. What are you up to this beautiful Saturday?" Mom glances at me with a smile and offers to make me some breakfast.

"No, please don't make a fuss over me. I just came by to say hi. I wasn't trying to be creepy, but I was enjoying watching you two just be."
"Are you sure you're alright, Eden?"

I laugh and wave a hand at her, "Mom, I'm good."Yes, she's been good. She wants to visit in the next few weeks with Davis." After college, Callie moved a few states over so she tries to visit every couple months. She moved for a job and wound up meeting her fiancé, Davis. I chew on my nail trying to find a way to bring up running into Noah. "So, I ran into um, Noah the other day…" I look up to see my mom's face. she asks." "How did that go?"

"It went well. I actually met up with him last night to catch up." I pause before continuing. "I told him about James and vice versa."She nods her head as if she knew that was the right thing to do and would have said so if I hadn't volunteered the information myself. "That's good. Best to be upfront with your relationship before he gets his hopes up."

"Mom! What are you even talking about? Noah and I have always just been friends," I point out. I mean, she knows there was something when we were teenagers, but that was ten years ago. We're adults now, and things change. Granted, I know how he feels, and judging by the look on her face right now, she already knows how he feels, too.

"Oh honey, that boy has always had a crush on you. Michelle and I used to talk about it all the time when the two of you would play all day until the streetlights came on, and we had to bribe you back inside. To be honest, we always thought the two of you would end up together. That is before everything happened, that is."

I place my face in my hands and lean on the counter. "Mom. We aren't kids anymore; things change." But even as I say those words out loud, they sound forced.

"I know things change. But there's no time stamp on it. You can think you're headed one way and wind up on a completely different path.

Take your dad and I for example." Dad looks up briefly to acknowledge he's somewhat listening, then Mom continues on with her point. "We never would have met had we not gone to the same university. I almost went somewhere else and changed my mind at the last minute. Call it fate or coincidence, but things happen for a reason. We like James. He's a wonderful young man and treats you well. But…" she stops and looks down at the spot on the counter she's been wiping for the last five minutes. "Maybe running into Noah after all these years is a sign. Have you thought about your feelings there at all?"

"Yes, I have. Of course, I have. I just spent three hours at the pub with him last night catching up, and it felt like we never lost touch. But one night of catching up isn't reason enough to end a two-year relationship." I toss my hands in the air like I'm fed up or surrendering. It's hard to decipher which one I'm aiming for. It's almost as if I've been trying to convince myself to stay in a relationship that while good, is also lacking in some ways. I never gave it much thought because I've been content, but I don't just want to be content. I want to be in love.

Mom looks at me with a soft expression and comes to sit next to me, abandoning the spot on the counter. She brushes my hair back behind my ear, something Noah always did, and sighs. "Look, I can just see it all over your face that James isn't the one you want to wake up to every Sunday morning. The one you want to travel with, start a family with. He's always been a sweet guy, but no one, and I mean no one, has ever looked at you the way Noah Rivers does. You can try to brush it off, but it's there. Look at yourself in the mirror, and it's there sweetie." I called my mom the morning after I ran into Noah at the café. I told her everything I said that day, so hearing her root for us in a way is strange.

In the midst of her little speech, I hadn't realized I was crying until a tear slipped off my chin and onto my hands. I stare down at it and realize I know what I need to do. Being with James has always been easy, predictable. But Noah coming back into my life has opened my eyes to something more. I would be doing myself and James a disservice if I stay in that relationship.

Mom wraps me in one of her hugs and squeezes me tight, reassuring me it's all going to be okay without even having to say so. We both laugh when we feel Dad reach over and wrap his arms around the two of us. When I came by this morning, I didn't know I would be deciding my future with James and Noah all at once. If I thought this revelation was hard, then the conversation I need to have next is sure to be a doozy.

14

AGE 14

I didn't sleep all last night anticipating seeing Noah again. I wasn't expecting my first kiss to happen Saturday night let alone with Noah. Having that break in our friendship for a year and a half had me thinking we could never get back to the way things were and definitely not to what we started last night.

I walk to the bus stop and see Noah immediately. He's smiling at me, and I feel my heart beat out of my chest. After all these years, this is finally happening. We held hands on the bus on the way to school, talking aimlessly about Halloween and Christmas break in a few months. Everything felt easy with Noah, like this is how we were always supposed to be. There was a crisp cinnamon-scented breeze wafting in through the bus windows, blowing my hair around lightly and tickling my neck.

I was so distracted by the sound of Noah's voice and the way his lips moved that I didn't even see it coming. One second, we're riding to school, and the next all I can hear is a loud ringing in my ears. I try to open my eyes, but there's dust filtering in and stinging them closed. I feel around for Noah, but I can't find him, all I feel are sharp little shards digging into my palms. My side hurts, there's a throbbing in my head, and I can barely hear someone yelling my name.

Noah? Why are you yelling at me, what happened? I say to myself. I can hear him, but he sounds so far away. I'm trying desperately to open my eyes, but suddenly I feel tired, and the thought of keeping them closed sounds better right now. *I'm cold, Noah, I just want to stay here for a little while, okay?* I keep telling him that I'm cold, but he's not listening. He keeps telling me to move, but I don't want to. I want to stay here where it's warm. I don't feel the breeze coming through the window anymore. I only feel the hot sun on my skin, keeping me grounded to where I am. I hear him yell, *"EDEN!"* one more time before everything goes quiet.

A few days later.

Our school bus had skidded to an abrupt stop to avoid hitting an oncoming car whose driver had lost control of their vehicle. I wasn't aware of any of this until an hour ago when Mom and Dad told me I was in the hospital with a concussion, a broken arm, and several broken ribs. When the bus tried to stop, it hit a tree and it pitched, along with everyone in it, to one side. I was on the side with the most impact. Noah landed on top of me crushing my ribs. Almost instantly the bus caught fire and was half engulfed in flames when Noah managed to yank me out. I don't remember anything, just that we were discussing our favorite Christmas movies, then everything went black. That was three days ago.

Noah only suffered some scrapes, based on what Mom told me. I wouldn't know, since he hasn't come by to see me yet. I'm sure he's shaken up by the accident, considering he remembers more than me, but still, I want to see him. His parents, Michelle and John, came by with some flowers yesterday, and when I asked about him, they just smiled and said he was resting. They assured me he would come visit soon. But something felt off. Noah should be right by my side, and he's not. If this were him lying in a hospital bed, I would be here for him.

So, why didn't he want to be here for me?

I hate hospitals. There's always someone coming in and out of the room, machines beeping, and these awful gowns. My head hurts, and I start to fade out again when I hear Mom whispering to who I can only assume is Michelle.

"He isn't coming today? Did you tell him she really wants to see him?" Mom nods her head slowly and then covers her face with one hand before speaking through it. "Michelle, he needs to understand there was nothing he could have done to prevent it. It's not his fault he landed on her..." she stops to listen again. "Okay, I'll tell her." She hangs up the phone, sits down in a chair by the window and cries.

I haven't heard my mom cry since she burned our turkey last Thanksgiving. We were supposed to have the whole family over, and she was already nervous about hosting. Dad told her we could fix it and still have a great Thanksgiving. He ran to the store and managed to get everything for tacos. We laid all the toppings out on the table like a taco buffet, and to this day, it's still the best Thanksgiving we've ever had.

Noah isn't coming to see me, not today and not anytime soon. I can already tell just by looking at Mom. Instead of asking her, I just close my eyes and try to sleep. If he doesn't want to be here then fine, that's his choice. But I'm not going to sit around and wait either. One night I had my first kiss and the real possibility of a relationship with Noah, and now I don't even know where we stand.

15

NOW

'**D**eep breaths Eden, you can do this.'

James comes over Sunday morning, exactly a week after Noah came back into my life and changed everything. The worst part about all of this is not only did I not see it coming, but neither will James. He doesn't deserve what I'm about to do, but even if I hadn't run into Noah last week, this is the right thing.

He knocks lightly on my door and pokes his head in when I tell him it's open. As if I'm wearing a red warning sign, he takes one look at me and nods his head. My eyes are puffy from crying, and my hair is in a messy knot on top of my head. I'm still wearing sweatpants and an old high school T-shirt with a few holes in it. I have never felt lower than this moment, and James can see it all over my face.

"Hey, is everything okay?" he asks cautiously before taking a seat opposite me on the couch. "You've been crying," ee points out, and I just close my eyes and nod. "It's Noah, isn't it?" He speaks those four words, and I lose every bit of control I thought I had. My chest heaves, and I start blubbering like a woman who just got left at the altar.

"James, I'm so sorry. I don't even know what to say. I wasn't expecting any of this. But, Noah, he's just always been my best friend.

Even when we weren't on speaking terms, no one could ever really fill that space he left in my heart. I know that sounds like something from a movie script, but it's the truth. I buried my feelings for him so long ago, or at least I pretended to, that I didn't even know they existed anymore."

I take a few deep breaths trying to calm down before continuing again. James, always so considerate, has nestled closer to me and is lightly rubbing circles against my back as I try to tell him everything on my mind. I take a steady breath and look up at him. His piercing blue eyes are looking right into mine, and I swear I can see him working to understand and accept everything I've already told him.

"E, it's okay. I've always wanted what's best for you, and if that's not me anymore, then we both deserve to find what is. Does this hurt? Yeah, like a bitch." We both laugh because we both know how rarely James curses. "I love you Eden, and the last two years with you have been amazing, but we both know deep down this probably wasn't a forever thing, and that's okay."

I snuggle into his chest and just let him hold me for a while, knowing this is the last time we'll ever have this. God, I hope he finds the kind of woman who recognizes him for all that he is. Had I not given my heart away a long time ago, I could see my life with James. But like he said, deep down we both knew this wasn't it. We stay on the couch together for a while, talking about our favorite memories and how much we did together over the past two years. We're ending a relationship, but it also feels like we're starting a new friendship.

"James? What are the chances we can stay...I mean if it's not too weird, maybe we could..." I look at him to rescue me from my awkwardness, and he laughs lightly.

"Yes, Eden. I think we can still be friends, just maybe not right away, okay? As much as I understand where you're coming from, it's still going to be hard to see you."

"I understand that. Let's make a promise to check in every few months to see how the other is doing. Is that too cheesy?" I ask.

"I think that sounds just cheesy enough." He says with a soft peck to my forehead. A little while later, James heads out, and it isn't until after I close the door and breath in deeply that I notice the feeling of relief wash over me. That had to have been one of the easiest and calmest breakups in history. Aside from my blubbering mess of tears, it was calm and peaceful. Another example that this just wasn't right anymore. What I really want to do now is call Noah. But I don't want him to feel like a rebound. A few days to myself to collect my thoughts wouldn't hurt. I need a large glass of wine, maybe two.

After finishing off a bottle of wine all by myself, I pull my phone from my robe pocket and type out a text to Noah. One I will likely regret tomorrow, but Midnight Eden doesn't care.

"Noah. I can't stop thinking about you."

"I know that's probably too forward but whatever. There it is."

"I broke up with James tonight, just thought you should know."

"Meet me at the pond tomorrow morning if you're free."

16

AGE 16

Last week we celebrated my sixteenth birthday. I can hardly believe that. Mom must have said the same thing at least twenty times up until I blew out the candles on my cake after dinner. Callie came home from college to celebrate, which was nice. I don't get to see her as much anymore. It's not like she's that far away, but a two-hour drive for someone who doesn't have a car seems like a lot to ask of their parents. Callie still has her car Mom and Dad got for her, though, so she's able to come back whenever she can.

It's been almost two years since the accident, and things with Noah never went back to the way they were. He never came to the hospital, and he never checked up on me when I got home. I cried for days trying to understand what I did wrong to make him stay away like that. But after a few weeks I stopped caring altogether. This isn't going to be like last time where he cut me out without any explanation, and I just went crawling back like a little girl. I couldn't keep waiting for him to figure his shit out, so I moved on.

The summer between sophomore year and junior year I started dating Ryder. I'm sure that knowledge hit Noah square in the face, and if I'm honest with myself, I hope it did. That same summer Noah's dog,

Syren, died. I was upset about it,. He was honestly the coolest dog I'd ever met, so I can't even begin to understand how much it hurt Noah. Mom insisted we send a condolence card with a fresh baked apple pie. I signed the card but refused to drop it off. Callie brought it over instead, and when she got back she told me Noah's younger brother Charlie answered the door, not him. As if I cared.

I felt bad about Syren, but it wasn't enough of a reason for me to go and try to fix things between us. Maybe that makes me a shit person, but abandoning your best friend after a traumatic accident kind of makes him one, too.

Ryder and I have been dating for six months now, and he's the only thing that keeps me distracted long enough. There's a tree near my house that we like to go to that's hidden just enough from the street. Every day after school he meets me at our tree, and we make out for a while. I never knew kissing could be so much fun. With Noah, we only got the one kiss before the accident happened, so I never got to fully experience a true make out session. I know kissing can only last so long before Ryder starts asking about other things, but I'm happy with the way things are right now. I'm in no rush.

After the cake, I got to open my presents. Mom and Dad got me a new iPod with more storage so I can download even more music, and they also got me a gift card to the bookstore. Callie got me a really pretty sweater from a local boutique near her school, and Ryder got me tickets to the Jack Johnson concert coming in a few months. It's been the best birthday I've had in a while; it doesn't even make me miss Noah at all. Well maybe just a little…maybe.

17

Now

It's been four days since James and I broke up. I keep waiting for a wave of sadness to hit me, but it never does. I'm not sure if that makes me feel better or worse. The morning after the breakup I woke up to a text from Noah, and all my memories of the night before came rushing back. I told him about the breakup, and I told him I can't stop thinking about him. God, that's embarrassing. To my surprise, though, he was sweet and supportive. I had forgotten about asking him to meet me at the pond until he mentioned that he was on shift so he couldn't. Probably for the best considering I was slightly hungover and had bags under my eyes from crying so much.

We agreed to meet up this week, though, and the thought makes me nauseous and excited. I haven't had it in me to fill the girls in about everything that's happened, and since I'm seeing them tonight for our weekly wine night, I decided to just wait to tell them in person.

Later that night, we all sit around the island in my kitchen eating cheese and crackers and talking about taking a trip to the vineyard soon. As I'm uncorking the second bottle of wine, I decide now is as good a time as any to rip off the Band-Aid. "I broke up with James Sunday morning."

I let the confession hang in the air and look up to see Stella holding her wine glass mid sip, Emmy just staring at me, and Chloe letting out a whistle followed by,"*well shit.*" I pour myself a large glass of wine, take a big sip, and just shrug my shoulders. "It was time. Seeing Noah made me realize my relationship with James wasn't right anymore. He deserves better than that, and so do I. I don't want to stay in a relationship just because it's familiar and easy."

They're all quiet for far too long, and I wait for one of them to disagree with me and tell me what I did was wrong. But they don't. Chloe comes over to stand in front of me, grips my shoulders, and says,"I'm proud of you, E. You did the right thing." Stella and Emmy look at me and agree with a nod of their heads.

I feel a sigh of relief rise in my throat and let out a small laugh. "So, what do I do now?" They all exchange a glance and then look back to me at the same time as if they telepathically said the same thing to one another. Chloe gives me a serious look and simply says, "It's time for you to get your second chance."

Later that night.

There's a light knocking at the door, and I jump. Even though I knew he was headed over, I'm still not prepared. I had texted Noah and asked if he wanted to come by after his shift—to my surprise, he responded yes immediately. As soon as he said that, I all but hurried the girls out of my apartment so I could tidy up and then shower again when I worked myself into a sweat. Any other time, they would have ignored me and kept hanging out, but one look at my face, and they got the hint.

I had just finished getting dressed when I heard him at the door. I glance at my reflection in the mirror in the hall, take a deep breath, and reach for the door. It opens quietly, and I'm suddenly struck by the scent of Noah's cologne again. I have to find out what he wears. It's intoxicating. I motion for him to come inside and shut the door behind him.

He looks delectable, and I'm aware how weird that sounds, but there's something about the way he wears his hair now. Slightly long on top but shorter on the sides, it's a darker brown than when we were kids, but his eyes are the same hazel green they've always been. I used to love the way the sun hit his eyes just right and brought forward the dark green flecks in his eyes. Of course, I never told him that because he probably would have laughed and called me a weirdo. Can't say I'd blame him. He's much taller, too, at least six-three, and broader. Noah was always fit in high school. I guess that's what happens when you play three varsity sports. But now he's built like a man, not a teenage boy. His arms are wider than my thighs, and through his fitted heather gray tee, I can see his sculpted back muscles. My mouth waters just thinking about what he feels like underneath his clothes.

As if he can sense my distraction, he reaches out to graze my arm. "Eden, are you okay?" he asks softly while looking me directly in the eyes. I feel like for the first time in years I can truly look deeply into his eyes without feeling self-conscious that he's going to catch me staring. I blink as I look down to where his hand is still caressing my arm, and a cluster of goose bumps rise when his fingers linger.

"Yes," I whisper. "I'm just glad you're here."

"Me, too." He drops his arm slowly, grazing my arm all the way down as he does. As soon as his hand falls back to his side, I take the opportunity to lean in and wrap him in a hug. We stand like that for several minutes, and I listen to the sound of his heart beating in his chest rapidly.

"Your heart is beating so fast," I say, and he laughs, the feeling vibrating against my ear resting on his chest.

"I'm a little nervous, I guess," he finally admits as he pulls his head back to look at me. "I didn't think I'd ever get to hold you like this again. Since, well, you know..." He trails off quietly.

I do know. Because for years I pushed the thought of Noah to the back corner of my brain. To a place I could hide him away most of the time and only pull out the memories when I felt I could handle them. Sometimes thinking about everything we had, or could have had, hurt too much. So, it was better to just not think about it. It was easier that way.

"Maybe we should sit." I finally say as I pull out of his embrace and head for the couch. He sits down next to me but not so close that we're touching. We're both nervous and obviously unsure of how to behave in this type of situation. A big part of me wants to just cuddle up to his side and be best friends like we used to be. But the other part of me realizes I don't know Noah as an adult.

Things could have changed in the last four years since I've seen him. And, even then, we didn't really get to talk. That night in the bar was the first time I laid eyes on him in five years. After everything fell apart, he and I didn't speak for years, and the next thing I knew, their house was up for sale. I have so many questions about that, but tonight probably isn't the best time to bring up all the sordid details of our past.

I offer Noah a drink, partly because my mouth feels drier than an Arizona desert and partly because I need something to do other than awkwardly sit next to him wondering what to say. He accepts my offer, and I grab two ginger ales from the fridge before joining him on the couch again.

"How was your girls' night?" he asks, clearly remembering me mentioning it the other night.

"It was good. They came here this week, but I kicked them out when I knew you were coming by."

He looks at me with an apology on his face, ready to voice it when

I cut him off.

"I wanted you to come, so please don't look sorry I asked them to leave. I'd rather spend time with you anyway." I shake my head slightly. "Sorry, that was probably too forward. I'm rusty, as you can see."

"I'm no better, Eden, believe me. My body feels like it's on fire sitting here next to you. I don't know whether to go outside and get some fresh air or…" He stops before finishing his sentence and mutters a quick, *"Sorry, never mind."*

"What? You can say it." I wait for him to finish and add, "Please, Noah." He twines his fingers together and rests his elbows on his knees before continuing.

"Look, you just broke up with someone you had a relationship with for two years. The last thing I want to do is rush you or come in here making statements about how much I want to kiss you. Which I do, believe me. I really, *really* do. But I feel like we're finally getting our second chance, and I just…I don't want to ruin it…again." His voice grows soft as he finishes that last part, and my heart shatters at the memory of what happened the last time we took a chance. I barely survived it, but that was a long time ago.

Noah is right, this is our second chance, and I don't want to look back and regret not going for it. It takes me all of two seconds to think it through before I'm off the couch and kneeling in front of him, gripping his hands in mine.

"Noah…" He looks up at me, and there's a war of emotions in his eyes, but it settles the second he sees me lean into him slowly.

He unclasps his fingers, releasing mine as he slowly places his hands on either side of my face. I'm almost certain I stop breathing as he grazes his nose against mine, and I feel his breath against my lips. He smells like cedarwood and mint, and the scent goes straight to my head making me dizzy. After what feels like an eternity, Noah drops a soft kiss on my lips, keeping it gentle until I react. A little moan escapes from my parted lips, and he takes the opportunity to deepen the kiss. I push his shoulders back against the couch and swing my legs on either side of his lap so that I'm straddling him. I lean the front of my body into his and grip his hair in my hands pulling him closer to me as his tongue parts my lips, and I let him invade my mouth.

Suddenly our movements become more rushed, and I can't get enough of his taste. I grind my hips into him as he grips the back of my thighs and drags me even closer to him. He groans into my mouth and squeezes my backside, making my core ache with need. I haven't been touched like this probably ever. James was always so gentle and predictable with our sex life; this feels like something more. Desperate. I arch my back, tilting my head back, and Noah lowers his mouth to my neck, nibbling and sucking on it lightly. I squeeze his shoulders, and my body starts grinding against him seeking some release. I'm panting heavily as he palms one of my breasts in his hand, the other still gripping my ass.

He drags his mouth back to mine, and I bite his lower lip, him rewarding me with a deep moan before sliding his tongue against mine. We're both out of breath, and he pulls back to look at me. "So beautiful," he says as he traces his thumb over my red and swollen lips. "But we should probably slow down."

Everything in me wants to protest, to rip his clothes off and beg him to take me right here on the couch. But we both know that's not how this should happen. We need to do things right this time. I slide my hips back just a little and nod my head.

"You're right. We just got carried away."

I laugh, and he leans back in to kiss me gently.

I let his soft lips move over mine with perfect precision and try to commit this moment to memory. I plan on reliving it a few thousand times. My eyes are glassy, and my breathing is still a little shaky, but slowly I pull myself back into a seated position next to him. I lean my head on his shoulder and breathe in his scent again hoping some of it lingers on the blanket draped over the back of the couch. He wraps his arm around my shoulders and holds me quietly while his breathing returns to normal. I feel his lips kiss my forehead, and quietly he whispers, "Finally, our second chance."

18

AGE 16

We were two months into junior year when I noticed the sign in Noah's front yard. A very big part of me wanted to run over to it, rip it from the ground, and demand some answers. But I couldn't do that. We still haven't spoken since the accident, and I gave up trying to understand. I moved on. I started dating Ryder and put that part of my life behind me. So why does it feel like my heart is being ripped from my chest at the sight of a *For Sale* sign?

When I walked into my house, I shut the door behind me a little too hard which made Dad poke his head around the corner. "You okay, Edie-Pie?" The fact that he still uses the nickname he gave me as a kid softened my anger a little, and I slumped my backpack to the floor before walking over to him.

"What's up with the for sale sign in front of the Rivers' house?" I asked, even though I clearly could see they were selling their house and moving. My intent was clear, though—why the hell were they moving?! It surely couldn't be because of what happened. If it had been then they would have moved right after, right? It's been two years, so there must be another explanation.

"You should ask your mom, sweetie. She was on the phone with Michelle last night, so I'm sure she heard their reasons." Dad turned his attention back to the score he was writing for the class he's teaching at the university.

Apparently, his intuition isn't as good as Mom's because I'm really bothered by them moving, and to him, it's not a big deal. I rub my hands roughly over my face and walk to the kitchen to grab a glass of water. Where were they moving? Are they going far away or just to another house in town? Would we still be at the same school? God, there were so many things I wanted to ask but just couldn't.

I put the empty glass in the dishwasher and headed upstairs to my room. I flop onto my bed and stare at the books lined up in rainbow order on my bookshelf. I'm not OCD or anything, but I love organizing things by color. My books, the clothes hanging in my closet, and I even color coordinated the snacks in the cupboard last year.

Noah couldn't be moving away; he's my best friend. Well, he *was* my best friend before he shut me out...*again*. Maybe when he kissed me the night before the accident, he hadn't felt anything and just didn't know how to break it to me. He probably realized we were only meant to be friends but made things weird by kissing. Now the sight of me makes him sick, and that's why he ignores me completely. I clutch the fuzzy pillow on my bed and bury my face just as a sob breaks free from my throat.

I'm such an *idiot* to have thought he liked me. What if Ryder feels the same way? What if he was dared to ask me out, and it's all a lie? My body starts to sweat as I work myself into a panic. My chest feels tight and like I can't get a lungful of air into my system. I climb off the bed and start pacing the room as I shake my hands out a few times. I can feel sweat beading at my hairline, and my mouth is so dry it feels like cotton. I run to the bathroom to splash water on my face and brace my hands against the sink. I don't even want to look at myself in the mirror. I can't.

All my insecurities are bubbling to the surface, and if I chance a glance at my reflection, I'll spiral even more. I'm heading down a rabbit hole. I can feel it in the way my breathing is shallow and labored. Just call me Alice. I don't want to feel this way, I don't want to be another girl who is insecure about herself and starts changing everything to make others like her more.

I wish Callie were here. Not something I often think about, but I know I could talk to her about this. Mom is great, and I know she would listen, but she'll just try to soothe me and tell me I'm beautiful and perfect the way I am. Moms are too biased when it comes to their children, and right now, I need an honest opinion. I rush back downstairs to grab my phone from my backpack and take the steps two at a time back up to my room. As I sit down on the edge of my bed, I pull up Callie's contact information and select FaceTime. It rings for several seconds before her face comes into view. "Hey Eden, what's up?"

"I need some honest advice, and I know if I asked you to be serious, you would tell me the truth. Right?" I ask her in as serious of a tone as I can muster through my inner panic.

"Of course. Let's hear it." She waits for me to ask, and it takes me a minute to find the right way to say it. I finally just blurt it out and hope she doesn't laugh. "Am I ugly? Like, do you think I'm not that pretty, and Ryder is only dating me for ulterior motives? Cal, do not laugh. I could not be more serious right now." She looks at me through the phone, and honestly, she looks kind of angry, which I can't understand. I know she'll either give me the truth, or I'll be able to tell if she's lying. I wait impatiently for her to respond as I jiggle my leg up and down causing the phone to tremble a little.

"Eden, did Ryder say you aren't pretty enough for him? I'll fucking kill that little shit. I don't have classes until tomorrow afternoon. I'm gonna drive home right now, and..." Before she can finish her rant I stop her, "Callie, no! He hasn't said anything like that. I'm having an internal meltdown right now and started spiraling at the thought that maybe Noah stopped talking to me because he realized he didn't have feelings for me and just didn't know how to let me down easy. That led to thinking Ryder only started dating me because of a dare or something. I couldn't even look at myself in the mirror because I was too afraid I'd see all the potential ugly things Noah saw in me." A tear escapes and slowly cascades down my cheek and onto my leg.

Immediately, Callie's face softens when she realizes there's no actual threat to me. "Eden, you can't be serious right now." She speaks calmly and sincerely. "I need you to listen to me because I will be one hundred percent honest with you. You are so beautiful. I've always been a little jealous."

I for sure think I heard her wrong because I always thought Callie was the prettier of the two of us. I've always been shorter and rail thin with barely any curves my whole life. While Callie has killer boobs and actual curves. It's no wonder she always had boyfriends in school.

"You have long golden hair; it's always reminded me of Princess Aurora's hair in *Sleeping Beauty*. You don't cake your face in makeup, covering up your ivory skin and the light freckles dotting your nose. You've got prettier eyes, and your lips are fuller than mine. Any guy would be *lucky* to even be seen with you, let alone date you."

I take in everything she's said and feel another tear slip free. She's really being honest. I can tell. If she was lying, her right eye would twitch slightly—that's always been her tell. Granted, we're speaking on the phone, but I can still see her clearly enough to know her eye isn't twitching.

"Noah is an idiot for letting you go. And maybe in his mind he has his reasons, but Eden, those reasons are not your problem. If he couldn't see you for everything you are, then he doesn't deserve another second of your time or another tear. Promise me you won't keep putting yourself down because of something that shouldn't even be on your radar after two years."

I process everything she's said and promise to at least try. Being a teenager is tougher than I thought, and now I feel bad I never noticed if Callie went through this at sixteen.

"They're moving," I tell her calmly then continue. "I saw the sign out front today on my way home from school. I can't believe they're actually moving, Cal. What if I never see him again? I don't even know where they're moving to. Honestly, I don't even know why I'm letting this bother me so much." A laugh slips out, even though none of this is remotely funny.

"Because you care, E. You've always cared. It's not a bad thing, but caring for Noah Rivers is sort of your kryptonite. We both know that as mad as you are at him for everything that's happened, if he came over right now to talk, you'd listen. It's just in your nature to care, and that's amazing, E. It is. But I think it's time you free yourself from the hold Noah has on you. You deserve better."

I nodded in agreement and let those words soak in before thanking her.

We hung up a few minutes later, and I lay back on my bed staring up at the sticky star lights I hung when I was eleven. Noah helped me stick them to the ceiling, and we both had a crick in our necks for the next two days. I love those stars, but looking at them right now just makes me angry. I jump up and start picking them off the ceiling aggressively with my nails. By the time I get them all off, they're scattered all over my bed and floor.

Fifteen minutes later, every single star is in the trash can. All but one. I don't know why I kept it—maybe as a reminder for whatever reason. But I stick the star in the back of my diary and place it back on my shelf. Slowly but surely, I'm going to remove Noah Rivers from my life completely. If only it could be as easy as taking down those stupid stars.

19

NOW

After kissing Noah, everything inside me ignited. We kissed, *after ten years.* An entire decade has passed, and despite knowing that, it feels like we kissed for the first time just yesterday. At fourteen, I never expected that kiss we shared, and I certainly didn't expect what came after. I have so many questions I want to ask Noah, to finally have some answers and clarity. But the other part of me is scared to know. In some ways, it's better to just move forward than keep dwelling on the past.

I grab my bag and laptop and head down Lydon Street to the café. I haven't been in a few days due to my breakup with James and Chloe coming by with lattes for me. When I open the door to the café and hear the familiar bell ring over the door, I see Jules look up from the cappuccino she's making. "Eden! Where have you been, girl? I was starting to worry you didn't like my lattes anymore." She smirks at me knowing there's no way that's why I haven't been in and returns to making the cappuccino.

"Never. If there's one thing I can promise you, it's that I will *never* get sick of your caramel lattes—they're perfection." I grab a table by the window and pull out my laptop to start my work. Some people probably wouldn't want to work in an environment like this, with all the noise, but I find it helpful. I can't focus as well when it's too quiet. It makes every tiny sound that much more distracting. With a constant flow of noise, it kind of acts like a white noise machine.

I'm making headway on my story about the animal shelter in town and am halfway through my latte when I get a text from Noah. Last month, the animal shelter held a charity event to help raise money for the renovations they are planning in the coming weeks. The building probably hasn't been updated since the seventies and needs some major help. Most of the walls have either old wallpaper or paint that is chipping. They also have plans drawn up for an expansion to the back of the building for more kennels.

I was there to cover the event and seriously considered adopting at least five of the dogs. Someday, when I have my own house and hopefully some land, I'll rescue as many dogs as I can. Hopefully, I marry someone who is on board with it because after seeing the faces of those dogs in kennels, my heart is invested in helping as many as possible.

I slide my laptop back on the table before closing it and focusing on the text from Noah. My skin tingles at the memory of our time on the couch the other night and how much I desperately want to do it again. The whole rest of the night I could still feel the grip of his hands on my hips as I moved my body against his. If that's what it felt like just to *kiss* him, I don't know how I'll ever survive more. My skin was ablaze from his touches, and I still had all my clothes on. Something tells me one look from Noah, and those green eyes could make me come.

Shaking the naughty thoughts from my head, remembering I'm still in public and not at home, I open the text.

Noah: The other night was…amazing. I know this is last
minute, and probably too soon…but I have a wedding
this weekend up in New Hampshire.
Will you be my plus one?

A weekend away? With *Noah?* Will we be sharing the same room and possibly a bed? My heart rate starts to accelerate at the idea of that. I can feel something brewing low in my belly, and it's clear I need to pack up my shit and get home. Jules and I are cool, but I doubt she'd be okay with me being openly turned on in her café. My fingers fumble as I try to stuff my laptop back in my bag. Jules sees me rushing and walks over to me with a questioning look on her face.

"Everything okay over here, Eden?" she asks while scratching the side of her head in confusion. I must look like I'm having a fit or something, and she's unsure of how to approach.

"Oh, yes! Sorry I just realized I'm late for something and need to head out. Latte was amazing as always, Jules." I awkwardly pat her arm as I stroll past her and out the door. The air feels crisp, and I breathe in deeply trying to refocus my brain. It still seems crazy that he has this effect on me. I walk home slowly enjoying the breeze on my heated skin. A few minutes to think about my response will hopefully help me respond coolly and collected.

I've always loved fall—the crisp scent in the air and the falling leaves. People have always said Christmas is *"the most wonderful time of year,* "but I disagree. Feeling the leaves crunch beneath my feet mixed with the cold air brings me a kind of peace I don't get anywhere else.

I'm coming up to the pond when I feel my phone vibrate in my bag. I take a seat on the bench—the same bench Noah and I sat on the night I told him about my uncle. The same night we went home and watched Pleasantville, and the same night he kissed me for the first time. How can years go by and so many things change, and yet this bench has been here all that time? The same bench in the same spot at the same pond. I finished high school, went off to college, and moved back, all while this bench has sat right here.

Something about that constant has me feeling nostalgic and weirdly emotional. God, I hope they never get rid of this bench. It would feel like losing a loved one. I know that sounds crazy, but I'm a sentimental person, and even though that was the last night before shit hit the fan, this bench still holds so much meaning. I've been back to the pond plenty of times over the years, but truthfully, I have never sat on *this* bench again. This is the first time in a decade that I felt like I could.

I pull out my phone and see another text from Noah and smile. I read it and instantly feel bad. It's been almost an hour since he sent the first text about this weekend. I was so absorbed in my walk home and my appreciation for the damn bench, that I forgot to respond.

> **Noah: It's too soon to ask that of you. I'm sorry. There's just no one else I'd want to go with.**

I can feel a blush bloom across my face as I read it a second time. There's still so much we need to learn about each other and who we are as adults. We have so much history, and somewhere in my brain, there's a part of me that's screaming this is too soon. A weekend away together, especially if we share a room, could rush what we're trying to build. I don't want to risk going too fast just for us to burn to the ground again. I'd like to think we're mature adults and can handle our impulses, but I'm not naïve. I can either agree to go with him to the wedding and see what happens, or I can stay home and wonder what I'm missing.

It doesn't take a rocket scientist to solve my dilemma. I begin typing a response to Noah, already wondering if it's the right choice. Despite my inner monologue reminding me to think it through, I hit send and shove my phone back into my pocket. I'm only halfway through my draft for the charity event, and I need to call Roxanne, the head coordinator of the animal shelter, for a few quotes. There are at least three loads of laundry piled up in the wicker basket near the window in my room and a dishwasher full of dishes. Yet having a few more peaceful minutes watching the leaves fall gracefully to the pond's surface is the only thing that feels pressing right now.

I've spent the last decade just trying to get through each day, never really enjoying what's in front of me. There has always been a hole residing inside me, a hole that, no matter what I did or who I spent time with, could not be filled. Noah has brought a sense of belonging back into my life that I had assumed was long gone and buried. It's a big leap to end a solid two-year relationship and fall back into something with a guy who has bailed on me *twice* with no explanation.

I'm the girl in the movies everyone calls an idiot for falling for a guy who's no good for her. But the thing the movie never shows you is the raw and real moments behind the scenes. They don't show you the workings of your inner makeup longing for the other part of your soul, the person who makes you believe in soulmates. Noah's mom, Michelle, and my mom always used to joke about the two of us ending up together, saying we were inevitable. So much has happened to separate us in the last ten years, and somehow, we always find our way back.

This could all be another setup for failure. Another attempt that leads to nothing but us becoming estranged again. But no matter how many times things fall apart with Noah, I will *always* want to give it a second chance.

20

AGE 16

There's a moving truck in front of the Rivers' house. I have an insane urge to walk up to it and kick it. But that would not only result in a broken toe or two, but me looking like a jackass. Two things I don't feel the need to accomplish at the moment.

The house was officially listed for sale three weeks ago, and they've already accepted an offer. For a few days I tried convincing myself it was just a joke, that they weren't really selling the house. But Mom told me yesterday they accepted an offer and were packing up today. I'm watching the movers carry out furniture and boxes, like ants in an assembly line. These strangers walking out of a house I've spent most of my childhood in, carrying furniture that I've laid across looking at comic books with Noah while eating heaping bowls of ice cream that ultimately led to a stomachache. The computer chair we sat in making playlists for each other with our favorite songs. I still have mine, and something tells me Noah does not.

Years of memories are just being carted out of that house like they never even happened at all. Suddenly, I feel like I'm ten years old again with a stomachache from overeating ice cream. I refuse to cry. I will *not* cry. I chant it over and over, hoping I can convince myself to hold it together. I can feel my control slipping when I catch a glimpse of shaggy brown hair.

Noah emerges from the house carrying a box labeled *"Noah's stuff"* when he pauses. Goose bumps creep up on my arms, and I hold my breath for a second or two. As if he can sense me watching him from the window, he looks down at the box in his hands before slowly turning his head slightly to the right and right into my bedroom window. I hiccup and rush backward right into my dresser. Logically, I know he probably didn't even see me, but he looked right at my window.

What the hell did that even mean? He hasn't shown any sign of caring in the last two years. Now he's moving away, and he feels the need to glance at my room. Was he hoping to get some closure from a damn windowpane? Or was that some weird way of trying to conjure me into view just so I can witness him look away in disgust? Fuck. That. I fling my bedroom door open and barrel barefoot down the stairs and out the front door in seconds. I'm walking across the front lawn when an arm reaches out and pulls me back.

"What the hell?" I yell as I swing around to see my sister standing there gripping my arm with a warning look on her face.

"Eden, what do you think you're doing? Storming over there isn't going to accomplish anything." She releases my arm but steers me back in the direction of our house. "If anything, you look like you just escaped an insane asylum." She laughs, but there's no humor behind it.

"I have a few things I'd like to say to that asshole, and you're not going to keep me from doing it." I start to turn and make a run for it, but Callie catches me, reading my mind.

"Eden, stop! This is ridiculous. Don't you remember what I told you when you called me a few weeks ago?" she asks me. Of course I do. I remember it perfectly because it's the mantra I've been trying to live by since. She continues, "Noah does not see you for everything that you are. He *does not* deserve another second of your goddamn time, Eden. It's time to let it go…you deserve more." She drops my arm and is ready to lunge in case I try to run again.

I stare at her face, taking in the furrowed brow and look of concern coursing through her deep blue irises. As much as this hurts, she's right. Storming over there to tell off Noah isn't going to do anything but hurt me more. It's like opening a wound on your leg that has started to heal but hasn't fully recovered yet. In the last two years, he has not *once* tried to make amends. Why should I bother? I'm not the one who abandoned him and decided we weren't friends anymore. He made that decision all by himself. It's time *I* decide for *myself.*

I nod my head at Callie and walk back inside the house. I go back up to my room and over to the window reaching up to close the shades. He's leaving, and there's nothing I can do about it. Watching them pack up and leave isn't going to change that fact.

It's two in the morning now, and I'm wide awake, staring at my starless ceiling. As much as I told myself earlier nothing has changed, I can't help but feel the sting of hurt. I bite the inside of my cheek to stop the flood of tears waiting to let loose and taste the metallic tang of blood. Getting out of bed, I reach for my bathrobe and head out into the hall. I haven't done this since I was a little kid, but right now there's only one thing I need.

I quietly open the door and slip inside slowly, careful to avoid the floorboards that groan when you step on them. I pad across the plush rug with paisley designs that has always reminded me of a Vera Bradley bag and kneel at the side of my parents' bed. Like a little mouse, I whisper for my mom, and her eyes open in a flash.

"Eden?" she whispers, and all it takes is one tear to slip free before she lifts the comforter and gestures for me to lie down. I cradle into her as the tears begin to fall. She lightly traces my back, whispering a calming *"shh"* as I slowly fade to sleep.

21

Now

My overnight bag is packed and sitting by the front door. I have a garment bag with three different dress options hanging from the doorway next to a bag of shoe options. In true Eden fashion, I am overthinking everything and can't seem to just pick one dress. At the rate I'm going, my nerves are going to cause me to burn a hole in the floor with how many times I've paced back and forth.

I sent Noah a text saying I'd be happy to join him this weekend, and I've been freaking out ever since. When I saw the girls last night, they all tried to help me get ready for two nights away with Noah. The result was in three dress options, a last-minute appointment to the waxer this morning, and an overnight shipment of lingerie. The last one was completely unnecessary, but Chloe insisted and bought everything before I could protest. As I was packing, Jack Johnson's "Constellations" playing softly in the background helping to keep me calm, I contemplated not bringing the lingerie. But Chloe and I have been friends for over twenty years, and she can *always* tell when I'm lying. She would undoubtedly ask me about it when I got back and would instantly know I was lying if I said he loved it. So, into the bag it went. I guess it doesn't hurt to be prepared.

By the time I finally sit down to settle my nerves a little, there's a knock at my door. I jump up and practically rush to the door before stopping to shake out my clammy hands and blot the sweat forming on my forehead. I never used to be this jumpy. My insides are buzzing like the bass turned up way too loud in a club and vibrating against my bones. I'm going to have to find a way to calm myself down, or this is going to be a *very* long car ride. Three hours when it comes to work is a drop in the bucket compared to the lake I'm about to swim across. What if we run out of things to talk about and an awkward silence settles over us? I tend to babble when I'm nervous and end up sounding like a crack addict who just snorted a line and drank three cups of espresso. Not exactly the impression I want to make on Noah's friends this weekend.

Telling my inner monologue to shut the hell up, I open the door to see Noah standing there. He's dressed casually, but the smoldering look in his eyes is anything but. He's wearing a pair of dark denim jeans with a thin, black, hooded Henley. His hair isn't as long and shaggy as it was when we were kids, but that little length on top and pushed to the side is the sexiest thing I've ever seen. Every part of me wants to lean in and run my fingers through it and yank his mouth to mine.

He can definitely tell what I'm thinking right now because he leans in slowly wrapping his arm around my back to pull me to his chest. His voice is a low whisper but deep with desire. "Eden, are you thinking dirty things right now?"

Busted. I can hardly breathe let alone respond to him. All I can do is hum in agreement. He chuckles, and I feel the vibration from his chest against my own.

"If you can't control your thoughts, then we're never going to make it out of this apartment. Which wouldn't be good, considering I'm a groomsman in this wedding," he adds, which is news to me.

"Wait, you're *in* the wedding? I thought we were just guests." A new surge of panic courses through me because if Noah is a part of the wedding, that means I'll be on my own for a good portion of the time. I don't know any of his friends. Hell, I didn't even know I would be attending a wedding until this week. As if sensing my panic, he places his hand on my chin to lift my face so that I'm gazing right at him.

"Eden, relax. The wedding is being held on the grounds of the hotel we're staying at. You can hang around the room or take advantage of the amenities while I'm getting ready. I promise the only time you'll be solo is for the actual ceremony. After that, I'm going to insist you stay by my side for the rest of the evening."

Releasing my chin, he leans in to place a soft kiss on my forehead. These little gestures are what keep me awake at night staring at the ceiling. We could have always had this, but instead we wasted *years* apart. I can hear Stevie Nicks clear as day singing, *"I know I could have loved you, but you would not let me."* All I ever wanted to do was love Noah. I just hope this time around, he doesn't disappear from me again.

Noah carries my bags down to the car and opens the passenger side door for me. I climb into his Jeep Wrangler and look around. As kids, we always talked about the cars we would drive when we got older, so it doesn't surprise me that Noah went with a Wrangler. The outside is a deep maroon color with black hubcaps and a roof rack on top. The interior is completely black on black, and I can't help but laugh. Black was always *my* color, and now it seems to be his, too. He walks around to the driver's side and gets in looking at me with a question. "What's so funny?"

"Oh, I just find it ironic that everyone gave me shit growing up for always wearing black, and here you are with a fully black car," I state flatly. He starts the engine and looks over at me as he places a hand on my thigh immediately resulting in goose bumps.

"The outside is maroon," he says with a shrug of his shoulders and a smirk that makes me want to lick his face. The heat spreading across my face is undoubtedly noticeable, so I turn my gaze out the window as Noah pulls out of my driveway.

Two hours into the drive we make a stop at a rest area to stretch and use the restroom. Noah finished before me and is standing in the checkout line when I come out of the bathroom. He finishes up, and we head back to the car to drive the rest of the way. I buckle my seat belt and reach for the bag with his purchases in it to place it on the floor by my feet.

"I grabbed you a treat if you're hungry." Noah gestures toward the bag on the floor. I retrieve it and open the bag to find at least a dozen Twix bars and nothing else. I'm staring into the bag when Noah clears his throat, "Twix is still your favorite, right?" he asks. I don't understand why exactly, but I feel tears building behind my eyes and quickly manage to shake them before smiling up at Noah.

"Yes. I can't believe you remembered that." For all he knew, I found a new favorite candy, or stopped eating Twix because I got sick of them. If he remembered this about me, it meant that he still cared, at least a little. My mind is running a million miles a second trying to understand how he could have walked away from me the way he did if he still cared.

His voice pulls me out of my thoughts. "Of course I remember. I remember a lot of things about you, Eden." He focuses back on the road, and we drive in silence for a while, only talking to trade off on music playlists. We're halfway through one of my picks when he asks me who sings the song.

"Stevie Nicks," I tell him and continue humming the tune in my head. When I look back over at him, he seems lost in thought. I want to ask him if he's okay, but Noah isn't one to offer up information when asked. He has to want to divulge his feelings.

"How many times have you listened to this song?" "I lost count, if

I'm being honest," I say with a laugh and look back out the window. The question is bothering me, though not in a bad way, but it seems like a strange thing to ask. "Can I ask why?"

Knowing what I'm referring to, he takes a deep breath and runs a hand through his hair. "I just wondered if it had an impact on you or something. I know that's weird, too, but the first verse is stuck in my head, and I can't help but wonder if it holds any meaning to you."

After all these years, he still knows me. He can still open the door to my heart, walk in blindly and know exactly where everything is. All the things that make me who I am, they've always been laid out to him, no barriers. I wish I could say the same about him, but there's still so much I don't understand, stuff I'm not sure I ever will. I have to wait to see if he's even willing to go back down that road and discuss our past.

"Well, I guess if I'm being honest, I listened to it probably a hundred times the day you moved," I tell him while looking down at my hands interlocked on my lap. I nervously rub my thumb up and down and wait for him to react to that confession. He'll know now why that first verse stuck out so much. I heard those words over and over in my head for months, and I couldn't resist crying each time. I kept asking myself, *"Have you forgotten me?"*

The last verse fades out and comes to an end. I handed the phone to Noah to pick the next song hoping to move past the awkward silence emanating throughout the car. But instead, he puts it down in the cupholder. I feel Noah shift in his seat before reaching across the console and taking my hand firmly in his.

"I didn't want to leave, Eden. I know it doesn't change anything, but I just thought you should know. I never *wanted* to leave you." Then why did you? The question is on the tip of my tongue, but the rational part of me knows this isn't the time or place to have this discussion. We're thirty minutes away from the hotel, and the celebrations will begin. This is the happiest weekend for one of Noah's best friends. Everything with us can wait.

I squeeze his hand in acknowledgment and offer a small smile. Turning my head back out the window, Noah reaches for the phone and puts on a more upbeat song. I didn't mean to bring down the mood, but maybe it was good he recognized those words. Maybe now he'll understand just a little of what I went through when he left. Even though Arctic Monkeys "R U Mine?" is pumping through the speakers, I'm still singing "If You Ever Did Believe" in my head. I swipe away a tear quickly before Noah has a chance to see. I allow myself one last memory of Noah walking down his walkway toward the moving truck before focusing on the breeze flowing through the open windows and the breathtaking sight of mountains in front of us.

"You've left me now, and it's seasoned my soul. And with every step you take, I watch another part of you go."

22

AGE 18

Being a senior in high school is everything I expected it to be, minus one thing. Noah isn't here. Once the moving truck disappeared around the corner that day, I locked myself in my room to cry alone. I didn't want anyone to see how upset I truly was, even though they could probably already tell. The only thing that softened the sting a little was learning they only moved two towns over. Might as well have been another continent, though, because whether they were right next door or thousands of miles away, Noah had cut me off from his life, and it didn't look like that would ever change.

The summer before senior year started Ryder broke up with me. I wish I could say I was devastated, but honestly, I didn't care all that much. I tried to convince myself I had true feelings for him, but really, he was just a placeholder, and even he knew it. Ryder and Noah used to be best friends, and when we started dating their friendship took a hit because of it. Noah was clearly bothered by it, but Ryder is a go-with-the-flow, laid back kind of guy with lots of friends. I don't think he cared that he hurt Noah, and as shitty as it is, I didn't care either. I wanted him to hurt the way he hurt me. I wanted to get a reaction out of him, *anything* out of him, but it didn't matter. He never said a word to me.

Instead, they packed up their house and moved thirty minutes away. My mom and Michelle stayed in touch the first few months, but after a while, they realized their friendship had only grown because of Noah and me. Once that friendship severed, the moms didn't see any reason to hold on either.

Within the first two weeks of school starting, Ryder found a new girlfriend, Jocelyn Clark. Honestly, she was a total bitch, so my only thought was *"good luck with that."* Being single felt infinitely better than being in a relationship, a feeling none of my friends shared with me. Chloe and her boyfriend, Lucas, had been dating on and off again since we were sixteen. Their relationship is as turbulent as a flight during a thunderstorm, but they always wind up back together.

She told me she lost her virginity the summer before senior year, a week before Ryder dumped me. It was weird to think we were the same age and had been best friends forever, and yet I had never felt more different from her than in that moment. I was happy for her since she was so happy, but I couldn't imagine losing my virginity to some guy who picked fights every other week. Chloe is a spitfire and can handle herself, but I wish she could see herself the way I do and give herself more value.

It feels like déjà vu when Chloe and I are perusing rack after rack of gowns for prom. It reminds me of the day we went to get dresses for the Valentine's Day dance. The memory is still so vivid in my mind I wonder if Chloe will remember it the way I do. I promised her that day that I would get a more colorful dress for the next dance. But as I stand here looking them over, I know wholeheartedly I will be purchasing a black gown.

After trying on thirteen dresses, Chloe finally decides on a gown. She emerges from the dressing room in a tight-fitting dress the color of the ocean with diamonds encrusted in the deep V-neck. It's nothing I would ever wear but fits her perfectly. If she hadn't already lost her virginity to Lucas, she would be tonight. I tell her that, and we both start cracking up before she looks back at me seriously.

"I already know what you're thinking, Eden, and I decided it's not my place to tell you what colors to wear." She pauses to pull her hair up and check out the back of the dress and how low cut it is. Her parents are going to *flip* when they see this dress, and that probably only makes Chloe want it that much more. "There's an elegant black gown in the dressing room for you to try on. If you don't like it, I won't be offended, but I saw it and just thought it was perfect for you."

She slips back into her dressing room to change, and I hesitate before going into my own changing room and locking the door. Without too much thought, I pull the dress from the hanger and slip it on. Looking in the mirror at myself feels like I'm watching a movie of myself but with someone else on screen. Chloe was right. This is the perfect dress. It's a strapless sweetheart neckline gown, black satin with a modest slit up the thigh. There's no bling, no dramatic plunge in the neckline, and I don't even think I'll need to have it altered. The dress slides down my body effortlessly, and the fabric pools at my feet.

I'm still staring at myself when Chloe knocks on the door and demands to see it. "Open up, E. I need to see if I was right!" I laugh while simultaneously rolling my eyes before opening the door to show her. "Are you fucking kidding me?!" she screams, and I slap her arm and tell her to keep her voice down.

"Eden! I am *SO* sorry for all the times I got on you about wearing black. This is your color, babe." Chloe hugs me tightly and starts gushing about how excited she is for prom this weekend. We're all going together in a limo our parents chipped in to rent for us, and most of our friends have dates. Truthfully, there was no one I wanted to go with. I'd rather just have fun with my friends. Chloe thinks I'll regret the decision later in life, but I already know I won't.

Prom day arrived, and Mom took me to get my hair and makeup done at the salon in town. It wasn't cheap, but a part of me suspected she did it because she felt bad I didn't have a date. I insisted that I, in fact, did not want a date and had been asked by three different guys.

I kept my hair simple to match the simple elegance of my dress and had the hairstylist use a large barrel curling iron to give me loose voluminous waves. The makeup artist did a smoky look with a little cat eye and dark red lipstick. I felt like Morticia Addams, and I loved it. The only jewelry I wore was a pair of long metal rod earrings that dangled just above my shoulders. I wanted to stay true to myself and keep everything simple, including my shoes, a chunky heel with transparent straps. But of course, I stashed a pair of Converse in my bag to change into for the afterparty along with sweats and a T-shirt.

I have the perfect view of my friends from the punch table, and I glance over my shoulder to see them laughing and dancing the night away. Admittedly I'm having more fun than I expected to, and it's a welcome surprise. As I finish my punch and drop the cup into the trash can, a song comes on and echoes throughout the banquet hall. I freeze, and my heart feels like it's crawling up my throat.

The DJ announces that this song was a special request when a few students groan at the old time music, but I can barely see straight. I'm fourteen years old again, lying on the floor wrapped in blankets next to Noah watching *Pleasantville* for the first time. Etta James belts out "At Last," and suddenly I'm bursting out the front doors seeking fresh air.

It's a humid night for June and the thick air clogs my throat, making me gasp just as a teacher comes out and sees me hunched over. She probably thought I was drunk and throwing up, but I assured her I haven't been drinking and that I just got overheated. I stand up straight and offer her a weak smile hoping it is convincing enough for her to go back inside. She lingers for another minute then decides to head back in. I walk over to the tree line where a single bench sits and take a seat. It looks nothing like the bench at the pond, but at this moment, with that song playing, all I can think about is Noah.

Lately it's been easier to push aside any thoughts of him since I haven't seen him in two years. But no matter how much time has passed, and no matter how much I try to convince myself I've moved on, I always get drawn back in somehow. Our souls are two magnets, fighting to stay away from each other on one side but fitting together perfectly on the other. A deeper attraction exists, and the harder I try to push it away, the stronger it pulls me in. I sigh into my hands as I rest my face against them.

23

Now

We arrive at a breathtaking hotel nestled in the mountains surrounded by nothing but nature. The privacy factor alone makes me like this place, but as we walk the grounds before heading to our room, I could see why his friend picked this venue. The wedding is a black-tie event and will extend through the whole weekend. Tonight is the rehearsal dinner, tomorrow is the wedding and reception, and there is a brunch Sunday morning.

Noah directs me to a small pond at the back of the property, and we make our way to the gazebo built over the water. The water reflects the already changing leaves, giving it a red glow. A few swans swim by, and the water ripples to the edge of the walkway leading to the gazebo. Being here reminds me of the pond back home, a place Noah and I haven't visited together again since that night ten years ago. I ask him as I take a seat.

"Honestly, no. It is too hard to even look at it when I have to drive by. The thought of going back there without you doesn't seem right."

It's hard to process things like this when Noah says them because for years, I convinced myself he didn't care about me. Now it's clear he feels the opposite. So how am I just supposed to change ten years of feeling rejected and not wanted?

"What did you mean in the car? About not wanting to leave me back then?" I know now probably isn't the time, but I just need to know. Before I get an answer out of Noah, someone calls out to him.

"Yo, Noah! Rehearsal is in an hour. Time to get ready, man," a tall skinny guy yells from the patio off the back of the hotel. I'm assuming the groom.

"Crap. I'm so sorry, Eden. That's Remi, and his bride-to-be, Alyssa, is a stickler for punctuality. We should probably find our room."

"Of course. Lead the way." I try to brush off my disappointment at being interrupted when Noah stops me to look me dead in the eyes.

"I promise we will have this conversation. There's so much I want to tell you. Okay?" He waits for me to respond while looking at me with a concern I can't quite place.

"Okay." I smile and let him lead the way into the hotel to find our room and get ready for the festivities.

The rehearsal and dinner went about as smoothly as these things can go. Only one of the groomsmen got a little too tipsy and passed out in a chair before dessert was served. I consider that a win. Noah and I head back to our room, and I'm so thankful to put on a pair of sweatpants and take off my heels. On my way to the bathroom to wash my face, I notice a piece of folded up paper sticking out of Noah's jacket. I know it's none of my business, but curiosity gets the best of me, and I slide it out to snoop. I only need to read the first line before realizing it's a best man's speech. He didn't tell me he was the best man, just that he was in the wedding party. He's perched on the end of the bed searching for a movie to watch, and I hold the speech out to him.

"Don't worry, I didn't read it." I smile, and he takes the pages in his hands looking embarrassed. "But why didn't you tell me you were the best man?"

He flips the folded pages over in his hands before looking at me. "Because I'm not sure the speech is even good, and truthfully, I didn't want to make a big deal out of it." He shrugs and walks back to put the speech in his jacket. Before turning around, he leans against the doorframe and sighs. "I wrote most of the speech before I asked you to come with me, and now...I'm just nervous to recite it in front of all those people I barely know and mostly in front of you."

His confession hangs in the air, and I quickly try to figure out how to reassure him it'll be great. "Noah, don't stress about reading it in front of strangers. By the time you give your speech chances are half the room will be drunk. And as far as reading it in front of me, I'm sure I'll think it's beautiful. You've always been good with words." I'm standing in front of him looking up at him from my five-foot-tall frame. When we were kids, our height difference wasn't all that dramatic. But standing in front of him barefoot now, the difference is almost comical.

I reach up on my tiptoes to wrap my arms around his neck and give him a soft kiss. I want him to feel comfortable with me and be able to talk about anything, including his speech. I try to give him a look of encouragement, but it quickly turns to a look of lust. He licks his bottom lip and releases a sigh as he wraps his arms around my back. Leaning my body into him and tightening my arms around his neck unleashes something in Noah. He quickly grabs me under my thighs and lifts me up until my legs are wrapped tightly around his waist. I can feel his length hardening against my stomach, and my mouth goes cotton dry. Carrying me carefully over to the bed, he sits down on the edge so that I'm straddling him.

"God, you're beautiful. Eden," he says as he trails soft kisses down my neck.

"I'm literally wearing a T-shirt and sweatpants," I laugh into his neck, and he continues his kisses down to my collarbone.

"I know. It's really sexy," he tells me before nipping at the base of my throat.

"Noah Rivers, don't you dare give me a hickey before a fancy wedding!" I push my body closer to him feeling like we're still not close enough, even though I'm straddling him.

"Fair enough," he says as he looks at me with a devilish smile. "Can I give you a hickey somewhere *besides* your neck?"

Heart pounding, I pull his bottom lip in between my teeth and bite down lightly, him rewarding me with a growl. One second, I'm straddling him in the power position, and the next I'm flat on my back, Noah looming over me with desire written all over his face. He uses one arm to prop himself up while the other travels down to my side, grazing my ribs lightly and then coasting in between my thighs. My legs tremble in anticipation, and I can feel my arousal gathering in my undies. I've never been so turned on in my life, and he hasn't even touched me yet.

Noah hooks a thumb into the waistband of my sweatpants and slowly starts pulling them down until they're gathered at my ankles. I kick them off and get a look at him just as he notices my lacy black undies. He curses under his breath and palms me through my underwear, feeling the heat radiating from the most sensitive part of me. I'm wriggling beneath him impatiently waiting for him to touch me where I need him the most.

"Patience, love. We've got time," he whispers into my ear as he traces light circles over my clit.

My back arches off the bed forcing his hand to press into me harder. This is new territory for both of us, the farthest we've ever gone before is a kiss, and we were only fourteen. I'm nervous and trembling, but it's from both nerves and desire. I need him more than I ever thought I'd need anyone. Noah looks at me for consent as he slowly pulls the fabric of my underwear down my thighs. God, *yes*. Completely bared to him I start to feel a crimson flush paint my cheeks, but I'm too in the moment to care.

"You're perfect, Eden." He pulls me into a seated position, lifts my arms, and pulls my T-shirt up and over my head. He lets out a quiet "*fuck*" when he sees I'm not wearing a bra. He lowers his mouth to one of my breasts and pulls the peak into his mouth and starts to suck gently. I inhale sharply and guide his hand back down to my aching, soaked center.

Losing all control, Noah pulls back and lowers himself in between my legs wrapping his arms under me and dragging me to his waiting mouth. He licks his tongue up the length of my slit, and my vision goes blotchy. He licks me again and pushes a finger into my heat.

"You taste amazing, baby. Like the sweetest honey."

Noah slides a second finger inside me and starts to suck on my sensitive nub. I can already feel an orgasm brewing, and he just started. I've never really been a fan of oral sex, but now I know it's because no one has ever done it like Noah.

He goes back and forth between light licks and rough sucking on my clit. Bringing me to the edge just to pull back, leaving me wanting more. "Noah, *please...*" I beg.

"Please *what*, baby? Tell me what you want," he teases me with his fingers, slowly sliding in and out of me making me see stars.

"I want you. Just you," I tell him. That's all the motivation he needs because he goes from soft touches to intense movements. Fingering me with such precision I can hardly speak. "Right there, *yesss*. Noah, don't stop. I'm close," I moan and arch my back slightly against him giving him even more access to my aching center. He curls a finger up inside me hitting a spot I didn't even know existed and immediately I'm spiraling. Experiencing one of the best orgasms I've ever had, I yell out his name. "*Noah*, fuck!" I scream. I start to come down from my post orgasmic high and look up to see him smiling at me. My face goes beet red, and I grab a pillow to cover it.

Noah reaches for the pillow, exposing me to him once again. "You don't have to hide from me, not ever. That was the most amazing thing I've ever seen. The way your body responds to me is like heaven." He pulls me to his side and spoons my body against his, Tracing light circles on my shoulder and showering my back with kisses. I don't realize how tired I am until I'm dozing off to the sound of Noah breathing right beside me. How am I ever going to go back to a life without him now? Noah is like a drug to me, and I'm addicted for life

24

AGE 18

Despite everything that's been thrown my way the last few years, I somehow managed to secure a scholarship to my dream school. When the envelope showed up one morning, I couldn't do anything but stare at it. In the top left corner, the familiar Columbia University logo held my attention for longer than I care to admit. I wanted to sit in limbo for just a little longer and hold onto the hope that I got in. I knew if I opened that letter and saw a rejection, I would crumble.

I distracted myself most of the day, finding anything to keep me busy, including cleaning the entire kitchen top to bottom. The look on my mom's face when she got home was worth it, though. Made me realize I should be doing more around here to help her out. After the shock of a clean kitchen wore off, she looked at me sitting at the kitchen table staring down at the unopened letter.

"Eden? Honey, are you going to open it?" she asked as she took a seat across from me.

I take a deep breath and look at my mom, "I'm scared. What if I didn't get accepted?"

She reaches her hands across the table and takes mine in hers.

"Eden, you are so talented, and regardless of the contents of that letter, your dad and I are *so* proud of you. You've overcome plenty of adversity in the last few years. Not getting accepted to this school will not define you." She squeezes my hand in a gesture to look at her. When I do, she continues. "You can do it, Edie-Pie." I smile at her using my dad's nickname for me and pick up the envelope. It's a small piece of paper, and it might as well weigh a thousand pounds.

With trembling hands, I rip open the envelope and slide the folded sheet out. One last deep breath, and I unfold it to reveal the trajectory for my future. The words are clear as day, but I can't bring myself to process their meaning. My mom is waiting anxiously across the table from me with an expectant look. After a few seconds I lift my tear-filled eyes to look at her."I…I got in." A tear slips free, landing on my acceptance letter, and my mom leaps to her feet in excitement.

"Oh Eden! I knew you could do it, honey. We are celebrating *big* tonight!" She gives me a tight hug before bustling out of the room to make reservations at my favorite restaurant. I can't believe I got in. The future I've always envisioned is becoming a reality, and as happy as I am, I can't help but wish Noah were here to celebrate with me.

That night we went to dinner as a family. Even Callie drove down with her new boyfriend, Davis, to celebrate with us. Lorenzo's is my favorite restaurant, and they have the most amazing garlic bread and basil-infused oil for dipping. After a heaping serving of fettuccine alfredo, we ordered dessert, and I was serenaded by the wait staff. Mom must have said something on the way in to let them know we were here celebrating, but as I look over at Callie and see her "cat that ate the canary" grin, I know it was her.

While Dad is paying the bill, out of the corner of my eye I see a young busboy approach our table. "Charlie! It's so nice to see you. We didn't know you worked here." My mom stands to greet him with a hug, and he smiles awkwardly. Charlie is Noah's younger brother who is likely sixteen now, and the resemblance between him and Noah is uncanny. I hadn't seen him since they moved, and then he was only thirteen and just starting to go through puberty. He's much taller now, not as tall as Noah and their father, but I have no doubt he'll shoot up even more. That whole family is tall.

"Hi, Mr. and Mrs. Walker. It's nice to see you all, too. What brought you to Lorenzo's?" he asks with a soft voice. Poor kid is nervous. I can only imagine what things he's heard from Noah over the years. For all I know, he painted me as the villain who abandoned *him*. Then again, Charlie was always the quiet one, something he gets from John. Michelle was always talkative and enthusiastic like Noah.

We make small talk. Mom asks how the family is doing since their move and how school is going for both Charlie and Noah. I cringe slightly when Mom gushes about me being accepted to Columbia, hence why we're here celebrating. Something tells me that news will get back to Noah by tonight. Good. Let him hear about my accomplishment getting into my dream school. Let him feel bad that he missed all of it and couldn't be here to celebrate with me. Let him realize I have been doing *just fine* with him gone and that all this time I didn't *need* him in my life. *Want* is a different story, but he doesn't need to know that.

Charlie clears our plates and promises to give his parents our best. As he starts to walk back to the kitchen, he glances over his shoulder and looks directly at me. I don't think he was expecting me to also be looking at him, and his cheeks flush when he realizes he's been caught. He disappears through the doors quickly, and I'm left confused and wondering what that lingering look meant. He didn't look disgusted or angry, something I sort of expected when I assumed Noah had bad-mouthed me. He almost looked sad. Charlie is several years younger than us, and our falling out happened when we were only fourteen.

There's no way he was affected by that at such a young age. I can't help but wonder what Noah might have said to him, how much he let him in.

On the drive home, I'm quiet and in my head as Callie and Davis gush about the first time they met. It's still early when we get back to the house, so I ask Mom if I can borrow the car and go to Chloe's house. Without hesitation she hands me the keys assuming I'm heading there to tell her about my acceptance letter. I feel a little deceitful, but I don't plan on going to Chloe's house. I plan on driving to Noah's.

An hour later I'm parked a few houses down and across the street from the Rivers' house. It's about the same size as their old house but definitely newer with a well-manicured lawn. A few lights are on in some of the windows on the first floor and only one light is on upstairs. I wonder if that's Noah's room. I can picture him lying on his bed, shaggy hair falling slightly in his eyes, and his hands behind his head. I wonder if he's going straight to the academy or if he plans to attend college first.

Before I even realize what I'm doing, I'm out of the car and walking up the front walk to their house. The porch light isn't on so I know no one will be able to see me, but still, I'm shaking. Maybe Noah will sense I'm here and come outside to see me. I'm lost in thought when I hear a car pull up to the sidewalk in front of the house. I scramble over to a bush to hide when I see Noah step out of the car followed by a beautiful brunette.

I know I'm breathing heavily, so I cover my mouth with my hand and watch them walk slowly up the walk. He looks just like I remember, only taller and more muscular. What I wouldn't do to feel those muscles, just once. Christ, Eden. This guy walked away from you without a care in the world. Now is not the time to be fantasizing about what his body feels like. I shake my head trying to rid my brain of naughty thoughts and lean in to hear them better.

"I had a really good time tonight. Thanks for coming with me," Noah tells the mystery brunette and leans in to hug her. My heart starts to crack when I see the two of them together, knowing this is his girlfriend and seeing how he gives her affection he could never give me.

"I had a really good time, too. I'm still nervous about what we did but definitely more excited now." She tells him as she pulls away and drops a kiss on his cheek. Everything in my body is screaming at me to run, go back to the car, drive home, and pretend this never happened. But I know if I try to sneak back to my car now, he'll see me. So, I keep my hand over my mouth to muffle the sob desperate to break free. I can feel it crawling up my throat, and I know once I let the emotions out, they're going to flood every nerve in my body. I just need to hold it together a few more minutes, then I can cry the entire way home.

The brunette walks back to her car, gets in, and drives away. Now is my chance to say something to Noah. Demand some answers. But what good will it do now? It's been years. He's clearly moved on, and so should I. As soon as I hear the front door close and lock, I jog back to the car and climb in with shaking limbs. My body feels like it's buzzing and not the good kind from excitement. Like every bone in my body is threatening to break and shatter me from the inside out. I really thought I had convinced myself I was past all this shit with Noah, when clearly, I'm just as affected now as I was four years ago.

Today was supposed to be an amazing day, a memory I'll never forget. I ruined it by coming here. Seeing them together has left a bad taste in my mouth, a taste that no amount of mouthwash is going to be able to get rid of. And I have no one to blame but myself.

25

NOW

Noah left a little while ago to meet up with the groom and other groomsmen to get ready for the wedding. The room we're staying in is beautiful with a large king-size bed that has the perfect view of the mountains. I walk out onto the balcony to get some fresh air and relax a little before I need to get ready. I brought several options with me to choose from for the wedding since it's a black-tie event, but on the drive up here I knew exactly which one I was going to wear.

I decided to curl my hair in thick loose curls before dragging it up into an elegant ponytail. I like the way my golden hair cascades down my back just a little, leaving the rest exposed by the strapless gown I'm wearing. I haven't even looked at this dress in years, but something about this moment felt like the perfect occasion to wear it once more. Noah has never seen this dress, something that bothered me years ago. I know he would think it was predictable, but I also know he would love it. At least, I hope he will.

I'm just sliding my heels on when I hear a knock at the door. I did my makeup like I had it done for prom—smoky eyes with deep red lipstick. I'm not sure who could be at the door, considering the only person I know at this wedding is Noah. But as I open the door to see him standing there in an all-black tuxedo with his hair expertly combed back, I lose my breath. He looks edible, and I'm almost tempted to pull him back into the room and show him just how good I think he looks. But this isn't my wedding day, and I wouldn't want to be the reason Remi's best friend isn't standing by his side.

Noah doesn't move as he slowly rakes his eyes up and down my body, taking in every detail. My eighteen-year-old self is dancing like a fool right now because of the way Noah is looking at me. I guess he does like the dress after all. There's something more in the expression on his face, though, more than just admiration. There's a dark desire behind those green eyes of his, and I have a feeling if we don't get away from this hotel room, we will likely miss the entire wedding. I step into the hallway shutting the door behind me. Best to eliminate the temptation altogether. "Well, don't you clean up nice," I say as I lay a hand on his broad chest. He grips my hand in his, drawing my attention to his face.

"You look absolutely stunning, Eden." He pauses, trying to tamp down whatever thoughts he's battling and gain some self-control. "If I thought it was even remotely possible to take you right here in this hallway, I would." He leans into me with a growl kissing me hard and desperate. I let all the air rush out of my lungs and suddenly feel a little lightheaded. The sexual tension between us right now is practically palpable. I lean into the kiss, wanting more. *Needing* more when Noah pulls back.

"We should head to where there are more people. I'll be able to control myself a little better knowing I can't strip you naked in front of a crowd."

That earns a chuckle as we head for the elevator. As soon as we step in, Noah closes in on me, caging me in the corner of the elevator.

"As soon as I can extricate us from this wedding, I am bringing you back here, stripping that gorgeous gown off your body, and devouring you."

My body stiffens, and I can feel desire pooling low in my belly. How can one sentence make me feel like I'm close to coming right here in a damn elevator?

I grip his lapels and pull his mouth to mine, bewitching him with a bite to his lower lip. His eyes roll back, and he thrusts his body into mine with a groan. Before he can say anything else, I look at him with mischief and say, "You promise?"

The wedding was enchanting, and the bride truly was the most beautiful bride I'd ever seen. I laughed at myself a little when I said that in my head because it reminded me of all the episodes of *Say Yes to the Dress* I used to watch. The consultants would tell every bride they were the most beautiful bride they'd ever seen. Alyssa wore a tight-fitting silk gown with a delicate and ornate lace overlay. The lace was dotted with tiny crystals that cascaded down her arms. She looked ethereal. I've only known Remi and Alyssa since yesterday, and I don't know a single other person here, but there wasn't a dry eye, me included, in this place. I've always wondered what my own wedding would look like someday and, more specifically, who I would be marrying. I glance up to see Noah looking right at me with a soft gaze. The look on his face makes me think he can read my mind and is imagining the same thing.

During cocktail hour, I mainly walked around the grounds taking in the beautiful scenery while the wedding party took pictures. I could see Noah and all the groomsmen laughing alongside Remi, presumably telling jokes to make the shots look candid. Alyssa took several with her bridesmaids before the entire group got together to take more. Once they're done, Noah strides toward me, beer in hand. "I need a little something to calm my nerves before my speech," he says, taking a sip.

"Well, for that we may need something a little stronger," I say gesturing toward the open bar. The bartender hands over two shots of whiskey, we clink glasses ,and I let the honey liquid slide down my throat. Seems like I need a little liquid encouragement, too, knowing what is likely to happen later tonight. A blush creeps across my face, and I turn to hide from Noah before he can read my mind and know exactly what I'm thinking about. I want him to focus on his speech and stay relaxed. I've never had to give a maid of honor speech, but now that my sister is engaged, I'm going to be giving one real soon.

After an incredible dinner of filet mignon, caramelized mashed potatoes, and veggies, it's time for the speeches. The maid of honor goes first and has the room equally laughing as well as tearing up. When the DJ calls Noah up, he squeezes my leg and drops a kiss to my cheek. "Wish me luck," he whispers as he strides up to the front confidently. Not that I would tell him this, but a part of me is nervous, too. No doubt he's written something about being in love and finding the right person, and I still don't know where he stands on those things personally. I give Noah one last encouraging smile and settle my nerves to hear his speech.

"Good evening, everyone. First, I'd like to thank everyone on behalf of the bride and groom's families for coming to this beautiful occasion. What a privilege to witness a love as honest and pure as Alyssa and Remi's," he glances over his shoulder to smile at them sitting at the sweetheart table.

"I've known Remi for nearly six years now since we started at the police academy together. We hit it off instantly and have been best friends ever since. We did it all together—the academy, the parties and going out, and everything after. All until he met Alyssa." The room laughs at his joke, he pauses before continuing. "Don't get me wrong. Alyssa is incredibly kind, giving, and good-natured. Not to mention she looks absolutely incredible tonight," he turns to smile at her and wink at Remi.

"Good work, Rem, you picked a good one. Not so sure what Alyssa was thinking, but hey." He shrugs his shoulders, and the gesture reminds me of when he was a kid and would say something funny like he knew he was a comedian.

Noah focuses back on his speech, more serious, and continues. "When Alyssa came into the picture, she started taking all of Remi's free time. I was honestly a little jealous at first. But, as soon as I saw them interacting more and falling in love, I realized I'd never want anything more for my best friend. To find a love so intoxicating, so real, everything else around you just fades away. Their love is something only a few people are lucky enough to find." Noah takes a breath looking down to scuff his shoe against the tile, clearly fighting the nerves.

"I believe in soulmates, that there is one person meant for each of us. Our bodies are just the vessels we have to keep our soul safe in until we meet the right person. When the right one comes along, it's undeniable. The gravitational pull you have toward them can't be denied. Even if you find yours when you're only ten years old." I gasp and look up at Noah just as a tear rolls down my cheek.

"Remi and Alyssa are two of the lucky ones, and I'm so happy you found each other." He raises his glass in toast and adds, "May the force be with you. Cheers." The room breaks out in applause as Noah makes his way back to our table. I'm swiping a tear away as he takes his seat next to me.

"Did I do okay?" But before I can tell him he killed it, he's pulling my face to his with concern. "Hey, what's wrong? Was it really so bad you felt the need to cry?" He tries to make light, but there's still that look of concern etched on his face.

"Noah, it was perfect. I'm tearing up because everything you said was beautiful. I can only hope someone says something sweet like that to me on my wedding day. If I ever get married that is," I laugh. I look up at him, and his face has softened a little. He wraps an arm around my shoulder lightly pulling me to his side when he states, "You'll have your day, I promise."

just seeing things, but just then he turns around. His entire face is on full display just feet away from me. He hasn't seen me yet, so I duck my head behind Chloe before he has a chance to notice us.

"Shit!" I try to whisper, but it comes out louder than I thought. My heart is pounding in my ears, and my hands are covered in sweat. Suddenly my feet feel like boulders, and my legs feel like Jell-O. Not a great combination when you're standing in between a bunch of drunk people dancing.

"Noah is standing over there with that group of guys we were looking at. I didn't know it was him for sure until he turned around." I'm babbling and talking way too fast, but somehow Chloe catches it all.

She starts to say something, but I interrupt and say I need to get out of there. Maybe some air will help to calm down my racing heart. Before she can offer to come with me, I'm pushing through the crowd of people trying to make my way to the door. I'm almost there when I bump into a tall, chiseled frame. I'm gazing down at my feet, and I don't dare look up for fear that I just bumped into the one person I was trying to escape.

"Is it really you?" he asks. God, that voice. Even after all these years, I could pick that voice out of the lineup instantly. I still can't look up, and I'm nervously swaying, debating on if I can make a run for it. "Eden? Look at me." But I can't. I've dreamed of looking into those eyes for so many years now. The second I look into them I know I'll crumble.

"I can't, I'm sorry. I have to go." I rush out the front door, past the bouncer and the line of people waiting their turn to get in. I'm such a coward. I couldn't even look at him, and now I've just humiliated myself and lost my place in the bar. Whatever, I should probably go home and take a cold shower or something anyway. I pull out my phone to text the girls and tell them I'm going home, but they should stay. I don't love walking home alone, especially at night in the city, but I'll take my chances if it means I don't have to face Noah.

"Eden, wait!" Noah yells from behind me, jogging to catch up. Fuck, I almost got away without having to do this. I take a deep breath and prepare myself for the conversation, which is now inevitable since he followed me out here.

When I turn around, I expect to see an older version of Noah, good looking as always and taller, naturally, because I swear the men in that family never stop growing. What I was not expecting to see was a muscular man with broad shoulders and no doubt an impressive six-pack under his shirt. His hair is short, like really short. From this angle it looks like he buzzed it, which is an odd sight considering Noah always had longer, floppy hair. He looks professional and put together.

Meanwhile, I've never felt like more of a mess in my life than this moment. I just fled from a bar to avoid seeing the boy who ripped my heart out and left without a backward glance. But gone is the little boy who stole my heart and never bothered to return it, and here I am the same little mouse I was at fourteen.

"Why did you run out like that? I can't believe you're really here." He's out of breath, which likely isn't because of the short jog over to me but instead because he's just as stunned as I am.

"I'm sorry, I just saw you and didn't know what else to do. Leaving felt like the safest option." I laugh, but there is zero humor behind it. I'm uncomfortable, and he can sense it.

"I didn't mean to chase you out here like that, but I couldn't just let you leave without saying hi." I cross my arms trying to appear unfazed, but every nerve in my body is hyperaware of his presence. "I'm not sure why saying hi to me now was so important.I sound harsh. I know I do, but I don't even care.

"I had a feeling you wouldn't exactly be happy to see me. Can't say

I blame you, but I'm so happy to see you, Eden. I probably don't have any right to say that, but it's true. It's *so* good to see you." He leans in and lowers his gaze to make eye contact with me, but I'm stubborn, and I refuse to meet it unless it's on my terms.

"What do you want, Noah? I'm not trying to be rude, truly, but please just tell me what you need so I can go home." I don't think I've ever sounded like more of a bitch, but at this moment it feels warranted.

"I don't need anything from you Eden. I just couldn't let you leave again." He goes to start talking again, but I've snapped. I cut him off and let him have seven years of hurt.

"*I* didn't leave, Noah. *You* did! The accident happened two days after we kissed, and you never came to see me! How the *fuck* was I supposed to feel after that? I laid in that hospital bed for *days* wondering what I must have done to make you abandon me. I cried myself to sleep every night for weeks thinking it must have been because you didn't like me and just couldn't find the words to tell me. Once I realized you weren't going to come back, I moved on. I *tried* to move on, that is." I'm breathing heavily and need to take a second to collect my thoughts, but Noah doesn't try to speak. He just waits for me to continue.

"Then I come to find out, you guys are moving. Selling your *fucking* house, packing up, and leaving. I had to watch you carry your things in boxes down to a moving truck that was taking you God knows how far away. Because *I didn't know* how far away you were going. There was no communication, no goodbye, *nothing*! I spent years thinking of ways to reach out, trying to find the right words to say to you, but I never could.

"Not until I drove to your house one night and saw you with a brunette. I hid in the fucking bushes like a goddamn stray cat. She was beautiful, and it made me hate her without even knowing who she was. As soon as she left, and you went into the house, I bolted to my car and drove home sobbing.

"So, tell me Noah, is this all you needed? Did you just need to hear how you broke me? I've spent years trying to piece my shit back together, and I gotta tell you, I've done a damn good job without you."

Noah reaches out to me, but I pull back and notice the look of hurt on his face. A part of me wants to hear his reasoning, but I spent far too many years desperate for an explanation. Right now, the only thing I'm desperate for is to get away from him. His smell is intoxicating, and I'm too vulnerable right now to trust myself, and my heart, around him.

"For years I prayed for you to come back and give me some reason, *anything*. I would have taken whatever you gave me back then, which is pathetic to admit. Right now, all I want is to do what you did to me when I needed you most. Walk away." And that's what I do. I turn around and head in the direction of my building, not even glancing back in his direction. I thought I would feel some kind of catharsis, but I just feel empty. I got out what I needed to get out, and all it left me with was a giant Noah-shaped hole in my chest.

27

NOW

We stayed at the reception until the last song faded out and said our goodbyes to Alyssa and Remi. We're all supposed to be meeting tomorrow morning for breakfast, but something tells me it'll be more like brunch. With every step we take bringing us closer to our room, my nerves increase a little more. Noah is holding my hand as we make our way off the elevator and down the hall. It's trembling a little, and I know he can feel it because he gives me a reassuring squeeze. "We don't have to do anything, Eden. I just want to be alone with you."

I'm so nervous to be with Noah on this level, but it scares me even more not being with him. We make it to our door, and before Noah can scan the card, I pull him into me branding him with a desperate kiss. "But you promised me I would be devoured." I gaze at him with all the seriousness and bravery I can muster, when in truth, my insides are screaming. In an instant the door flings open, slamming the wall behind it, and Noah is lifting me by my thighs, wrapping me around his waist. He kicks the door shut and walks me over to the bed before setting me down gently.

I can see the war of emotions he's fighting. Wanting to be gentle with me while desperately wanting to let the beast inside free. I release my tight ponytail and let my hair fall free. Noah leans in and slips a piece of it behind my ear. The first time he ever did that I nearly fell apart right in front of him, and right now is no different.

I can smell the faint aroma of whiskey on his breath, and all I want to do is drink in his scent and suck the flavor from his lips. He lowers his hand to caress my bare shoulder before his fingers linger at the sweetheart neckline of my gown. "Where did you get this dress, Eden?" he asks me with a sultry voice that goes straight to my core.

I take a shaky breath that ends up sounding more like a hiccup before I can answer him. "It's um, it's actually the dress I wore to my senior prom." I lift my eyes to meet his. "I know it's weird, but a part of me always wished you could have seen me wear it. Since it still fits, I just decided...I decided I wanted to wear it for you." My voice is breathy and soft because that confession suddenly makes me feel self-conscious and small.

He's looking at me with an unreadable expression, and I start to feel even more exposed. "Are you kidding?" he asks. "You wore your senior prom dress tonight because you wanted me to have a chance to see you in it"" My throat is burning, and I can't seem to get enough oxygen into my lungs. Was that a rhetorical question, or am I supposed to answer him?

"It's weird, isn't it? I don't even know what I was thinking." I plant my face in my hands and try to keep the impending tears at bay. This situation is already so embarrassing, I cannot start crying, too. Noah gently grasps my hands in one of his and uses the other to lift my chin so I'm looking at him.

"Eden," he whispers my name. "I have *never* been more turned on in my entire life than I am right now. The idea that you wore this dress for *me* makes me want to rip it from your body and take you over and over again, until you lose your voice and can no longer scream my name." He pauses to look at me and drops a hard kiss on my mouth. "That is the sexiest thing ever, Eden. *Ever.*"

Noah pulls me to my feet and slowly unzips the dress in the back, letting the silk material slip from my body and pool at my feet in a black puddle. He takes in the matching bra and undies set I'm wearing—a strapless corset style lace bra, completely transparent, and a matching high-waisted lace thong. The look he gives my body is like a man dying of thirst, and I'm the first glass of water he's had in days.

He drops to his knees in front of me and caresses the back of my legs all the way up to my ass. Squeezing it, he leans in to trail soft kisses up my thighs and to my stomach. I look down at him with hooded eyes feeling the desire pool inside me. I'm so wet I can feel it soaking through my undies, and he hasn't even touched me yet. As if reading my mind, he stands and slips a hand over my aching center and starts lightly rubbing. A moan escapes me, and I lean my head onto his shoulder. I start fumbling with the buttons on his shirt until his entire chiseled chest is on display for me. I use both hands to push his jacket and shirt off his body, and it thumps onto the floor.

I dig my nails into his chest hard as he continues his ministrations on my pulsing center. I want to feel him, *need* to feel him. I reach down to start unzipping his pants when he stops me. My breathing is labored and heavy, and a look of confusion crosses my face. Immediately he drags me flush against his body and devours my mouth with his. Pulling back only for a second, he says, "I promised to devour you, Eden. If you touch me now this will be over too soon, and I want to take my time with you." If there was ever a sexier sentence uttered in the history of the universe, I don't know what it would be.

Noah lowers me to the bed slowly and gently, as if I'm breakable. Never looking away from my face, he pulls my underwear down my legs and tosses them to the floor before taking a step back to drink me in. "You are so perfect. I've always imagined what it would be like to taste you." My eyes roll back, and I arch off the bed slightly, feeling the need for release in any way he'll give it to me.

"Is it everything you thought it would be?" I challenge him, thinking back to his mouth on me just last night. He grips both legs and bares me completely to him. Crawling onto the bed between my thighs he leans in and slowly licks me all the way from my backside to the top of my clit. I wiggle beneath him, desperate for more when he pulls back to stare at me.

"It's better." Without warning he buries his head between my legs and does exactly what he promised me. He *devours* every inch of me. I grip his hair and hold him as close to me as possible trying not to suffocate him. He plunges two fingers inside me stretching me in the most delicious way, and I cry out. Pumping both fingers in and out of me while lapping up everything I give him, I feel my orgasm waiting to detonate. All it takes is a curl of his finger in just the right spot, and I'm spiraling. Screaming his name so loud I can hardly hear anything over the ringing in my ears.

As I come down for the most intense orgasm ever, I look at him with a deep crimson blush painting my face. "Do you think our neighbors heard that?" I ask him quietly. "Oh, baby, I *pray* they heard that," he says with a devilish grin. "I'm sorry if I was suffocating you, but it just felt so good I couldn't get enough." I admit.

"Eden, I could die inside your pussy and think of no better way to go." He kisses me, and I taste myself on his lips—something that used to make me cringe, but this time I feel even more turned on. No one has ever worshipped my body the way Noah just did. I should feel tired after the night we just had, but honestly, I just want more of him.

"My turn." I smile at him as I flip over to straddle him. He starts to protest, but I cover his mouth with my hand. "Noah, I, too, have always imagined what you would taste like, what it would feel like to have your cock in my mouth." I reach for his buckle again and wait for him to stop me but finally he relents.

He lifts so I can pull his pants and boxers down his thighs, finally seeing him for the first time. My desire is clouded by fear for a moment when I see the size of this man. Noah has the most amazing cock I have ever seen, and the biggest. I bet if I asked him how long it was, he would know. All guys measure their dicks at least once in their life. I lower my head and encircle the head of his cock with my lips, sucking gently. I dart my tongue out and taste the salty moisture already beading on the tip. His head falls back against the pillows just as I take him all the way into my mouth. I suck the tip, applying slight pressure to his balls and working the length of his shaft with my hand.

Noah fists the sheets in his hands and moans something unintelligible while I work him faster now. "*Fuck*, Eden." I smile knowing I'm bringing this reaction out of him and keep working him harder. He grips my hair and pulls me off him as my mouth makes a wet popping sound. "I'm too close. That feels amazing, but I just need to feel you."

I reach around my back and unclasp my bra. Noah takes in the sight of my breasts and the twin peaks pointing right at him as if begging for his attention. He leans down and sucks one into his mouth, lapping at my nipple while kneading the other breast with his hand.

I arch my body and grind against his length feeling how slick I am against him. He abandons the first breast, leaving it red and puckered, and switches to the other. He sucks firmly, and I feel the pull deep in my belly desperate to feel him buried inside me. Noah reaches for his pants to retrieve a condom from his wallet.

"Are you sure?" he asks before ripping the foil packet open.

"God, *yes*." I moan against his mouth, sucking his bottom lip in between my teeth and biting down. He slides the condom on and positions himself at my entrance but doesn't enter me. I look at him ready to ask what's wrong when he leans in to kiss me so softly and sweetly.

"I've thought about this moment more than you can even imagine. I just need to make sure you're real." He caresses my cheek lightly with one hand while the other is holding his weight up above me.

"I'm here. This is real, Noah." I stare into his eyes and nod my head in encouragement. The tip of his cock slides up my opening once, twice, before *finally*, he slowly enters me. Feeling him sheath himself completely inside me is a mix of pleasure and pain. He's much bigger than I expected, and I can feel all of him stretching me to my limits. Yet, I still need *more*. I start moving my body against his, already feeling my release building within me.

"*Noah*." I moan his name and that only encourages him to keep moving. "I'm so full. You're too big." I admit even, though I don't want him to stop.

"You can take it, baby. You're taking my cock so well, *fuck*." He moans into my neck and nibbles the sensitive flesh. I can feel the palpitations in my chest and neck, and something tells me Noah feels it, too. "You're so wet, Eden. I don't think I can ever get enough of this tight pussy." He groans as he pumps into me with such force I scream into his chest. My face feels hot, and my entire body is likely flushed crimson. Just then, he rolls us so that I'm on top of him and in full control. "Ride me, baby."

Noah grips my hips tightly and pulls me impossibly closer to him. He's so deep inside me right now I can't tell where I end, and he begins. I start to roll my hips into him, setting a steady pace when I feel the orgasm blossoming. I plant both hands on his chest and use him as leverage to lift myself up just to come slamming back down on him. I repeat this again and again while Noah's grip on my hips tightens.

He moves one hand to my center and rubs my clit as I grind against him harder and faster now. "*Yes*, just like that," I breathe heavily and feel my body tighten just as I explode around him. "Noah!" I yell his name as I ride out my orgasm that seems to go on forever. He's still pumping into me, and the sensation is almost too much. It's so good I feel another orgasm threaten to consume me. I've never experienced sex like this, where I'm so desperate to be filled by someone. To be filled by Noah.

He abruptly pulls out and flips me on my stomach before entering me again with a hard thrust. I muffle loud moans into the pillow and let him fill me as his orgasm wrenches free. "Eden!" he yells loudly enough that the neighbors surely know what we are doing in here. I come again right with Noah, and I truly have never felt more connected to another person than in this moment.

Our bodies are slick with sweat, and now I'm imagining him taking me in the shower. He pulls out of me and discards the condom in the trash can. I roll onto my back, chest heaving, and he climbs back into the bed with me. "Are you okay?" he asks, pressing a soft kiss to my temple.

"Truthfully? I've never felt better," I tell him. "Which I know sounds cheesy, but that was the best sex ever, and I'm already wondering when we can do it again." I laugh and roll onto my side so I'm facing him.

"Trust me, that's the first of many times," he says. "I'm already so addicted to the feel of you wrapped around my cock, screaming my name as I fill you completely. It's the sexiest thing I've ever seen." I blush at his words and lightly trace my fingers around each cut ab muscle on his stomach. I wonder if he would think I'm a complete weirdo if I just licked him.

"What time is it?" I ask, looking toward the clock. "Holy shit, it's three o'clock in the morning." I don't even remember what time it was when we started this, but it's clear now my body needs sleep. We're supposed to meet the wedding party for breakfast in a few hours.

"Time flies when you're having fun," he says, and I laugh at his use of that idiom. I snuggle against his chest, and he pulls the covers up over our naked bodies. He wraps an arm around me and whispers something, but I'm already falling asleep so I don't even hear what it was.

28

AGE 21

"**M**an, I wish I was there to see that. You sound badass, E," Chloe says over the rim of her mimosa. I filled the girls in about the Noah debacle last night over brunch. Archie's is this awesome brunch place within walking distance that has the best food and killer mimosas. I was on my third glass by the time I relayed all the details of my public tantrum with Noah. As embarrassing as it was, I stand by everything I said. I've spent so many years trying to push aside all my feelings for Noah. Hurt, anger, even love for him. Last night I was presented with an opportunity to let it all out, and that I did.

Turns out Emmy saw Noah walk back into the bar, presumably to tell his friends he was leaving, with an expression best described as heartbroken. At least, according to Emmy. God knows how many drinks she'd had by then. For all I know, last night was the last time I'll ever see him and my only chance to tell him how what he did affected me much more than he realized. I doubt it'll make a difference, but in some ways, I think this was an eye opener. It's time I put our past in the past and really try to move on.

I'm a week out from my finals and graduation is in ten days. I've been so ready for this day to come, to be done with school and to focus on a career. But now that it's almost here, I don't feel ready. "m lost in thought, picking at my French toast when Chloe grabs my hand. "E, it's okay to feel how you're feeling. Last night must not have been easy, on top of everything you have going on with finals, graduation coming up ,and applying for writing jobs. Just promise me you won't shut down and handle everything on your own. We're here for you." She gives my hand a gentle squeeze before pulling Stella and Emmy in to give me a group hug. I want to laugh and cry. These girls have been there for me through so much, and as much as I'd like to say I can handle my shit on my own, I'm lucky to have them.

"What would I do without you girls?" I ask, smiling up at them.

"Well, luckily you'll never have to find out." Stella winks at me, while Emmy nods her head in agreement.

"Now, let's order another pitcher of mimosas!" Chloe declares.

I raise my glass to them. "Hear hear."

I'm studying for my finals when I see an incoming call from my mom. "Hey Mom, what's up?" I ask, somewhat distracted as I go over my notes.

"Oh, hi, honey. How was your night last night?" she asks, and immediately I know she knows what happened between Noah and I.

"How do you already know what happened?" I ask, skipping the bullshit. We both know she's heard, so we might as well cut to the chase.

"I'm not very subtle, am I?" I try not to laugh to spare her feelings. My mom is many things, but one thing she has never been is subtle. "I ran into Michelle this morning at the market, she mentioned you two ran into each other." Jesus, did he just run home to his mom to rat me out for yelling at him in public? I roll my eyes and mutter,"grow up" when my mom interrupts me. "Did something happen last night?

Michelle didn't say much."

"You could say that," I mutter. "I saw him at the bar last night, and he tried to talk to me like nothing ever happened between us. I kind of went off," I admit sheepishly, expecting my mom to scold me for being rude, especially in public.

"Good for you, sweetie," she says, and it takes me a moment to realize she's serious. "I've been wanting you to give that boy a piece of your mind for years. It's about time he hears it."

"I thought you were going to be disappointed and tell me to rise above it or something," I admit. "I was feeling a little embarrassed about it this morning to be honest." While I don't regret telling how I feel, I do hate that it had to be in public within earshot of thirty people. Whatever. It's not like I know any of those people anyway. "I still can't believe he told Michelle, though. Seems a little childish if you ask me."

"I'm not sure he did tell her. She never said," Mom says.

"Mom, who the hell else would have told her?" I ask her slightly exasperated. "I don't know, Eden; I'm just telling you what I know."

I don't mean to sound irritated with her, it's not her fault or anything. "I'm sorry, Mom, I'm not trying to take anything out on you. I'm just bothered by the whole situation. He appears out of the blue and says he just had to say hello, and it made me irate. What gives him the right to waltz over to me and try to have a normal conversation? He abandoned me and left without a backward glance. I can't just let that go and be like 'hey Noah, so good to see you!' Asshole." I gasp when I realize I just went on a rant and cursed over the phone to my mom. I'm not a little kid anymore. It's not like she can ground me for swearing, but still. I respect her enough to keep the bad language to myself.

Before I can apologize, Mom is speaking again. "He handled everything wrong, even Michelle admitted that to me once. But those are his burdens to carry through life, Eden, not yours." That takes me by surprise, and I process the words a few times in my head. They *are* his burdens, his wrongdoings, that he must live with. I no longer have the capacity to hold onto something that isn't mine to carry. I feel lighter in a way. Like I just lost a few pounds of heavy baggage weighing me down.

"Thank you, Mom. This actually helped a lot." I can tell she's smiling because if there's anything that makes my mom feel her best, it's when she knows she's needed.

"I love you Eden, and I'm so proud of you. See you in a few days for graduation." I tell her I love her and ask her to say the same to Dad for me and hang up. I'm going to focus on me, my career, and my future. Everything in the past can just stay there.

29

NOW

A phone is buzzing somewhere, but I'm too tired to check if it's mine. Noah shifts out of bed next to me and gets up. My eyes are still closed when I feel his body weight sink back onto the bed. I roll over to face him, taking in his light stubble and messy hair. It reminds me of when we were kids, always flowing freely and falling into his eyes.

"That was Remi. He said they're pushing breakfast back until eleven so everyone can sleep. Guess we weren't the only ones who stayed up late." He nibbles my ear lobe then turns my face toward him. "Last night was the best night of my life." He kisses me deeply, and already I can feel how much I want him.

"It's ten o'clock. Do you want to sleep a little longer before we need to head down?" Noah asks. "Actually, I have a better idea," I tell him with a smirk. I roll out of bed, still naked from last night, and saunter over to the bathroom door. "Care to join me?" I ask, motioning toward the shower. His face pales for half a second before he's launching out of bed and striding toward me, already rock hard. This might be the best shower of my life.

Noah turns on the water and gets it to a comfortable temperature.

Not scalding hot the way I like it, but something tells me we won't need the water to be too hot. I step in first, releasing a sigh as the warm water rushes down my body. I don't hear Noah join me so I open my eyes to see where he might have gone. He's still standing there just watching me with a dark expression.

"You have no idea how many times I've fantasized about you in the shower, Eden." I reach out to pull him in with me and rub my hands up his wet chest.

"I think I do. Right after I saw you that day, I fantasized about you touching me in the shower. Just like this…" I lean my back up against his front and guide one of his hands to touch my breast. Instinctively, he starts kneading it and pinches my nipple between two fingers.

"Did you touch yourself to the idea of me in there with you, Eden? Pretending it was my hands squeezing your breasts." He takes both in his hands and squeezes firmly. "My fingers fucking that tight wet pussy." Just then, he slips a finger inside me, and my knees tremble. One touch from him has me literally weak in the knees. A moan slips past my lips, and I grind back against him, needing more. "Tell me what you need, Eden," Noah says, while drawing his finger out and replacing it with two.

"More. I need *more*." I whimper and grind my back into him greedily, seeking the friction I so desperately want.

"I don't have a condom in here," he states and every part of me is begging him not to stop.

"I'm on the pill, and I get tested regularly," I tell him, praying he's not against going without protection. I've truthfully never done it without a condom before, but something about Noah has me dropping all the walls I spent years building. I grind my ass against his erection, and he groans into my neck.

"I'm clean, too. I've never done it without a condom, though. I'm not sure I'll be able to control myself once I get the feel of you, *just you*, sliding over my cock." Holy fuck. He can talk dirty to me day and night, and I'll be weeping for him each time.

"Neither have I, but I want you, I *need* you inside me Noah." He pulls my wet tresses over my shoulder to the side and bites into my neck while he guides the head of his cock to my soaking entrance.

"You sure, baby?" He asks. I respond by pushing against him so that the crest of him is pushing into me slightly. "I need to hear you say it, Eden." He's rubbing himself up and down my slit, making my vision tunnel.

"Y-yes, *please* Noah." In one movement, he thrusts himself in, and I'm impossibly full, letting out a yelp of pain and pleasure. He starts thrusting in and out of me slowly at first, then gaining speed. I place my palms against the cold wet tile desperately trying to hold on while he rams into me hard. I reach down and start circling my fingers over my clit delighting in the sensation mixed with the hot water streaming down my front.

Noah slows down a little and guides me forward by lightly pushing on my back. I lean forward to touch my toes so that my entire ass is on display for Noah. "Is this okay?" he asks while he slowly starts thrusting into me again.

"Fuck me harder." I say and slam my ass against him roughly to show him just how much I need him to let go. "I want to feel you lose control, Noah. Show me how much you need me." He only hesitates for a second before he's fucking me so hard the bathroom is filled with wet slapping sounds. The water is cascading down my head and into my face, but I don't care. I just want to feel Noah lose himself inside me.

I know he's trying to hold back so that I come first. So, I guide his free hand, the one not bruising my hip, to my center and push his fingers against me. Message received, because he starts skillfully rubbing my clit with such perfect precision that within seconds I'm screaming and letting the sounds of my orgasm fill the bathroom.

"Jesus, Eden. I'm coming." He grits out while slowly starting to pull out.

"Come inside me," I say and almost gawk that those words came out of my mouth. But honestly, nothing sounds hotter right now than him letting loose deep inside me. "I promise it's okay," I reassure him and he pounds back into me with a grunt and stills as he releases everything he has into me. The steam from the shower is fogging everything around us, and my vision is blurred from all the water dripping into my eyes. But there's no mistaking the way Noah sighed my name over and over as he came.

We towel off and get ready quickly to meet the wedding party downstairs for brunch. Our shower shenanigans took longer than planned, and as soon as Noah saw me trying to get dressed, we started all over again. It's crazy how I can't seem to get enough of him. We've had sex twice just this morning, and already I'm aching for him to be inside me again.

We made it downstairs to the lobby at exactly 10:59, which I felt was impressive considering how hard it was to leave the hotel room. The feel of Noah's hands on me is unlike anything I've ever experienced. Mix that with the delicious scent of him, I am practically making my mouth water at the thought. I'm a goner already.

Remi strides over to us with a brilliant smile. Surprising considering we went to bed just before the sun came up and knowing it was their wedding night, I assumed he and Alyssa did the same.

"Shit. You guys totally fucked last night, didn't you?" Remi says as if he were in the room to witness it.

"Jesus, Remi. We're not in college anymore. You don't just go around asking if people fucked." Noah sounds exasperated but also slightly amused, which causes a shy smile to creep across my face.

"Okay, then what would you say, Mr. Rivers? You two made love all night? Is that better?" He nudges Noah's shoulder knowing the answer is most definitely no, not better.

"We had a good night, alright? I assume you and the Mrs. did as well." Noah tries to shift the conversation off us and onto the newlyweds.

"Oh, you know we did. Hence why the brunch instead of breakfast decision was made."

The lobby is a beautiful open space showcasing the amenities around the grounds through big open windows. The foliage around this place is something I could easily get used to. Waking up to this amount of color just outside your window is a great way to start the day. We make our way to the dining room where the rest of the wedding party and family awaits. Everything around here smells like cinnamon. I'm tempted to ask if that's intended, or if it's just the way this place naturally smells. It reminds me of back home when Mom bakes her apple pies. The whole house ends up engulfed in that sweet scent.

"Good morning, you guys! How'd you sleep?" Alyssa walks over with an all-knowing grin on her face, wrapping me in a hug. Jesus, could everyone here tell we had sex last night...and this morning? I checked my hair before we left to make sure it wasn't crazy from the amount of times Noah had his hands in it. Every nerve in body tingled as his fingers expertly traced lines over every inch of me. I didn't check, but I'm almost certain Noah has some intense scratches down his back from my nails digging into him repeatedly.

I drag myself out of my thoughts and bring my focus back to Alyssa. "Yes, the bed was so comfortable. Honestly, I was so tired I would have slept anywhere." I laugh but can feel the strain in my voice. She can see right through me. I guess I'm not too good at sweeping things under the rug. "I bet you guys were exhausted, too." I try to shift the attention to her, but she's not having it.

"Yeah, the bed was great, the sex was great, but enough about me," she says.

"But you're the bride. This weekend should still be about you and Remi," I challenge.

"Listen, I know we don't know each other too well, but Remi and Noah are best friends. They work together, they hang out together, and honestly if they could, they'd probably shit at the same time." I get the feeling that the last part wasn't really a joke. "I've known Noah for several years now, and I have never seen him this happy. Something tells me you'll be sticking around." She gives me a knowing smile again, and I return it this time. I just met Alyssa this weekend, but she has this thing about her that just naturally makes you like her. She would fit right in with the girls. I might just invite her to our next wine night.

She can sense I'm in my thoughts again, so she tugs my arm bringing me over to her table. We sit down and wait for the boys to join us before our food is served. "You can be honest with me. The only person I'm likely to tell is Remi, and if I had to guess, I'd say Noah is filling him on everything already." She lifts her chin toward the guys standing in the back corner near the double doors that lead onto a deck overlooking the pond. They're standing close enough that they could be whispering or preparing to make out. Both thoughts bring a chuckle out of me.

"Thanks, Alyssa. This weekend has been so amazing, meeting you all and sharing your special day. Thank you for allowing me to be a part of it."

Sensing my inability to spill the details of last night, she drops it. We chat about the property grounds and how we both want to come back here this time of year next year. She even mentions making it a couple's trip. Alyssa has high hopes that this thing with Noah works out. I'd be lying if I didn't say I hope we can come back here a year from now as a couple, too.

Noah and Remi join us just as the server comes around with a tray of mimosas. I take a raspberry one and drink deeply. I'm not much of a drinker, but seeing Noah walk over in his dark jeans and Henley has my mouth going dry. "Parched there, Eden?" Noah teases me as he takes a sip of my drink from the exact spot my lips just touched. Why is that so hot?

I lick my lips before responding in his ear in a whisper. "Yes, my mouth is so dry from watching you stride over here looking so edible. Makes me want to take you back up to the hotel room and stay there the rest of the day." I drink the last of the mimosa as Noah makes a coughing sound and drinks half his water.

"Are you okay? You look a little pale, man," Remi asks, giving his shoulder a playful squeeze. Last night was just the tip of what's to come. Even though we spent the night together, and spent some time in the shower this morning, I feel like there's so much I still want to explore. Not just his body, but who he's become in the last decade. I'm always acutely aware of the elephant in the room, shoved in a corner and only slightly visible, but still there.

We've had such an amazing time this weekend. I really don't want to ruin it, but there are things we need to talk about before we can move on. Or at least, until I can move on. I have no idea where his head is at, so for all I know, he's unbothered by our past. It doesn't seem likely, but that's one thing that's always been consistent with Noah. I never know what to expect. Our time here is about to expire, and surely, I don't want to spend two hours in the car with him having a serious discussion when we can't even look at each other directly. As the chatter around the table continues while I've been in my thoughts, I decide this weekend isn't the time to dig up the past. Having this time with Noah, meeting his friends, and getting a glimpse into his world has brought a certain feeling out of me I didn't know was there. Maybe I can just let everything go and focus on the present.

I glance around the table at a group of people I hardly know all laughing together, telling inside jokes, and reminiscing over this weekend. I want to be part of this with him. I want to move in a positive direction with no barriers between us. As much as I wish I could just forget the accident ten years ago, and more importantly the aftermath, I need him to know how I felt then and how I feel now.

30

AGE 14

It's dark here, can someone turn on the lights? Nothing. I start feeling around for a light switch, but everything is rough, sharp, and weirdly hot. Are my eyes closed, and that's why I can't see? I focus hard on opening my eyes, but for some reason, they hurt. It feels like when you get an eyelash stuck, and no matter how many times you blink or try to make yourself cry, you can still feel it there.

Why can't I remember why my eyes hurt or why everything around me hurts? My side, it feels like I'm being crushed, and no matter how much I try to wiggle free, the pain just increases. This is the worst dream I've ever had, and when I wake up I hope I forget it. I try to move again, but something stops me, holding me in place. I start to panic, because not only am I blind, but now I'm being held down by something heavy. It's warm, though. That part feels nice actually, and even though I'm already dreaming, I just want to go to sleep. That's a weird feeling, wanting to sleep when you're already asleep. Dreams are funny like that, I guess. The pain, though, feels real, and I really don't like it right now. I wish Noah were here. *Noah.* He was right next to me just a minute ago, wasn't he? The bus! Oh god, we were on our way to school and the bus...this isn't a dream.

Things are coming into focus slowly, and that only makes the pain intensify. Someone is talking. I don't know what they're trying to say, but I can hear voices all around me. Quiet ones and some yelling. The one closest to me is screaming, and I wish more than anything I could reach out and slap whoever is being so loud.

"I'm tired," I try telling them. I just want to stay here and rest my eyes a little longer. The pain in my side seems to have gone away a little. I"s less intense than before, but it still hurts. The bus flipped, and I don't even know where we are, or where Noah is. I want to call for him, but I don't think I can. I try again to open my eyes, but dust fragments keep filtering in causing them to sting even worse than before.

I'm trying to calm myself down, but something smells weird, like fire but not the good kind with s'mores and hot dogs on a stick. The kind that makes me feel sick. I hear someone crying nearby, more than one person, I think. It's hard to focus right now because the main thing I keep hearing is this loud ringing sound. My head hurts, and I want to throw up, but I know if I move right now I likely will. Strong, warm hands are gripping me, trying to move me. He sounds familiar, but my mind is fuzzy again. I just want to go back to sleep and snuggle into the warm feeling next to me. Is that the sun? It's so much hotter than it was a few minutes ago when it was streaming in through the bus windows.

"Eden!" The voice yells at me again. Rude.

Can't they see I'm tired and don't want to be disturbed?

"EDEN!"

Oh god, it's Noah. Something is wrong...the bus! Fuck. I must have zoned out again. I need to get out of here. We need to get out of here. Noah, are you hurt? I need to see that you're okay. I can tell I'm not okay. My head is pounding and something definitely crushed me, but I just need to know that my best friend is okay. Noah...I...

It's black again. No sounds, no heat, and no warm arms pulling me out of the bus. He's gone, and right now there's nothing I can do about it. For days, I've laid in bed alternating between painful sobs that rack my bruised and broken body, and numbness. The dreams keep coming, reliving the nightmare repeatedly but in different ways each time. Somehow it always ends the same way, though. Me in the hospital, and my best friend nowhere to be seen.

Mom comes in every time she hears me scream. She must be tired, but no matter how many times I tell her I'll be okay and not to come running, she still does. One day I'll understand that feeling of loving another person so much you can't bear to see them in pain.

It felt like Noah and I were on that path, but clearly I was wrong. What the hell do I know anyway? I'm only fourteen. My ribs are still healing, which is great, but now that the pain of the accident is healing, it's replaced with the pain of losing my best friend. I just want to go back before the bus. Before all of it. I just want one more day with my best friend before everything changes. If only I was given the chance to go back in time, I could do things differently.

31

NOW

"Eden." A soft voice caresses me in my sleep. It sounds so peaceful I just want to go toward it like those fish drawn to deep-sea anglerfish. I'm in a trance listening to that voice, calming and serene, with a touch of concern. "Eden, baby. Open your eyes." God, that voice is like velvet against my skin or thick honey. Soft and sweet, the perfect combination. The voice is accompanied by strong warm hands now. Maybe this dream isn't so bad after all. This time my name comes through clear as day, and I open my eyes to see a concerned look on Noah's face.

"There you are," he says with a quick smile, before replacing it with that concerned look again. I return with a confused look of my own until he speaks again. "I think you were having a nightmare. I know I'm not supposed to wake someone abruptly, but you were starting to worry me."

"Um, what was I doing?" I ask, even though I remember the dream clearly. Nightmares from the accident still happen occasionally, but it's been a while. Seeing Noah, though a good thing, has stirred up some memories from the past. As much as I'm able to shove them aside when I'm awake, I can't control them coming through in my dreams.

"You kept saying, *'I just want to stay here where it's warm. I'm tired Noah.'*" I don't meet his eyes just yet, even though I feel them burning holes into the side of my face. He knows what I was dreaming about. He was there. But I don't want to talk about this at—I glance over at the clock—three o'clock in the morning.

"Sorry, sometimes I have nightmares. It's no biggie, though. I'm fine. Sorry I woke you." I lean over and place a soft kiss on his cheek before turning away from him.

"Eden, can we talk about this?" He asks softly, and the pain detectable in his voice makes me want to cry.

"Can we just talk tomorrow?" I ask. I can feel the tension rolling off his body in waves onto the bed sheets as if it's a tangible thing I can reach out and grab hold of. I roll back to lay my head on his chest and trace light circles across his abs. He smells incredible. He always does. Like sandalwood and something crisp. It makes me want to lick him, which given the circumstances, would be weird.

"I'm okay. I promise. And I promise we will talk about everything. Right now, I just want to lay here with you. Okay?" Noah wraps an arm around me and pulls me even closer to him. I hook my leg over his waist and squeeze. Tonight, we can just pretend all the bad stuff from our past doesn't exist. That can be tomorrow's problem.

My hair is piled in a messy bun on top of my head. My Warby Parker glasses are sliding down my nose even though I keep pushing them back up. And I'm still sitting in yesterday's pajamas. My article on the shelter is in its final stages, and I just want to make sure it's perfect. I've been so distracted lately, not that I mind, but I don't want my work to suffer just because I'm addicted to Noah's hands all over me. His hands, his body, that huge…Eden, focus!

I rub my hands down my face and get up to stretch. I just need a quick break to refocus and get back to work. I went shopping yesterday so I have all my favorite snacks and drinks. I make myself a grilled cheese sandwich with tomato soup, something cozy for a chilly day, and grab a ginger ale from the fridge.

I'm halfway through my sandwich when I hear a knock at the door. A glance at the clock tells me it's probably Chloe on her lunch break. Her office is down the street from my apartment, so it's not uncommon for her to stop by. I wipe the crumbs off my shirt and open the door, stunned to see Noah standing there looking perfect as always. A blush creeps across my face, and I glance down mortified by what I'm wearing. "Hi, I wasn't expecting you today. Clearly." I motion my hands over my body to emphasize if I had known I wouldn't look like a dumpster rat.

"You look beautiful as always, Eden." Noah leans in to drop a soft kiss on my lips. I close the door and follow him to the kitchen island where my half-eaten sandwich sits.

"Didn't your mom teach you that lying is bad?" I ask. "Actually, considering how well I used to know your mom, I know for a fact she taught you lying is bad." I perch myself on a bar stool and move my plate over so I can rest my head in my hands. My sandwich is still warm, but I suddenly feel self-conscious eating in front of Noah.

He walks over to my stool and spins me to face him. "Eden, one thing I will never do is lie to you." *Of course not, you'll just leave instead.* My inner Lizzie McGuire can be such a bitch sometimes. I can see her sitting there picking at her nails with a look of disgust on her face, judging me for trusting that Noah won't just up and leave without an explanation again. I like to think we've grown up since then, so I don't know why the voice in my head is always so negative.

I feel his hand graze my cheek and lift my chin so that I'm looking at him. He leans in and buries his face between my neck and shoulder inhaling my scent. A low growl vibrates against my neck, and I feel goose bumps dot my skin.

"Did you just shower?" The way he asks that has my panties dampening, and I don't know why it was so sexy, but it just was. I nod my head feeling a little dizzy with him in such proximity to me. "You smell amazing, Eden. Edible." He nibbles the soft curve of my neck, and a gasp slips from my lips as I course my hands up his chest. I fist his shirt and pull him to me so that he's standing right between my legs. Our lips are a breath apart, so I flick my tongue out just to taste him. His eyes roll back, and his grip on my waist tightens, dragging me forward on the seat until my core is pressed against him firmly. I have work to do, I know this, and yet I can't even find it in me to care right now. Noah is all-consuming. His scent, his presence, that impressive part of his body hardening against me, making my mouth go dry.

I lick my lips, and he catches my tongue between his teeth, teasing me gently as he bites down. I groan into his mouth and slip my hands under his shirt, feeling how muscular and perfect his body is. I guess being a police officer makes him eager to stay in good shape. God, if he wore his uniform here sometime, I'd probably drop to my knees and worship him any way he wanted.

The air around us feels thick, and all I can think about is wanting to feel him between my legs. I need him to touch me now, or I'm going to combust into flames right here in the kitchen. I've long forgotten about my grilled cheese, which is probably stone cold by now. The only thing I'm hungry for is Noah.

I lower my hands back down his chest and grab the hem of his shirt, lifting it up and over his head. His gaze burns into me as he watches me lick up his abs. I've been wanting to do that since the night of the wedding. I kiss and lick my way back up to his mouth before he kisses me with even more urgency than just a moment ago.

It feels like my underwear has disintegrated by now from the heat emanating from my core. As if reading my mind, Noah reaches down and starts rubbing circles over my center, causing my head to fall back. I start moving into his hand eagerly, needing more pressure, but he keeps his movements light. He's killing me, and he doesn't even know it. Or maybe he does, judging by the smirk on his face right now.

"Noah, I swear to god, if you don't touch me right now, I'll go do it myself," I challenge him, and he chuckles against my mouth.

"Mmm, as much as I'd like to see that, right now I just want to taste you. After all, this is lunch break, right?" He lowers to his knees, reaches for my shorts, and swiftly pulls them, and my underwear, down in one quick movement.

He grabs the back of my thighs and tugs me forward on the seat before resting my legs over each one of his shoulders. Slowly he starts teasing my entrance with little flicks of his tongue. After one minute of that, though, I'm writhing in my seat for more. "Are you just going to tease me until I die right here?" I ask with a somewhat annoyed edge to my voice. He laughs, and I feel his breath on me, causing me to shiver.

"I need to feel you, Noah, *please.*"

Apparently, I'm not above begging because I sound like someone starved and desperate. "As you wish." He smiles darkly. I can't even take in a lungful of air before he is back between my thighs literally *devouring* me. I squeeze my legs over his shoulders and grip his hair between my fingers, pulling not so gently. He probably can't even breathe right now, but the pressure is so delicious, I selfishly don't care. I have never been taken like this in such an urgent way. Like he needs me just as much as I need him.

I've always been self-conscious of guys going down on me, but Noah makes me feel different. He keeps up a steady speed and adds two fingers inside me, making my eyes roll all the way back. I'm grinding against his face like a nymphomaniac as my release crashes over me. I scream out so loudly my neighbors likely heard me, but I don't care. It's like whenever Noah is inside me, whether it's his skilled tongue or that impressive cock of his, I can't seem to care about anything else.

Rising to his feet, I can see my release glistening on his chin, and it makes me blush a deep scarlet. I hand him a towel to clean up just as he picks me up from under my ass and starts walking me to my bedroom. The second he rests me on my feet, my shirt is being lifted over my head, revealing my braless chest to him. He takes in my naked form and curses quietly under his breath. We don't waste another second before I'm undoing his belt and yanking him free of his jeans and boxers. I grab ahold of him and pull him to me gently by his erection before sliding it up my wet folds.

He grabs a condom, slides it on with perfect precision and is lifting me into his arms so that I can wrap all the way around him. He sinks down to the bed and guides my entrance over the head of his cock. I grip his muscles, reveling in the feel of how strong he is, and wait for him to lower me onto him. Painfully slow, he eases me down his length until I'm completely seated on him. The sensation is both almost too much and not enough. I start to grind against him, rubbing my clit against his pelvis for more pressure. Noah leans in and captures my mouth while squeezing me from behind, guiding me back and forth over him.

I can already feel my orgasm building low in my belly, and Noah reaches a hand between us to stroke me to my release. I'm grinding against him with such force that I can't even see straight. His muscled abs are rippling beneath me, and I know he's fighting for control. I love taking him to the edge and watching him shatter over how good we feel together. Seeing the look in his eyes when he comes, calling out my name like I'm the only one who can bring him to this place of desire.

My legs quake beneath me, and I'm spiraling. I'm flown into oblivion riding a high I never want to stop chasing. I keep coming, longer than I ever have, as Noah takes a nipple into his mouth sucking firmly. I'm gasping for air as my orgasm finally slows to an end, and I arch my back into Noah groaning at the friction between us.

"Fuck, you feel so good pumping in and out of me like that," I whisper into Noah's ear, nibbling it, and that's all it takes before he stills against me emptying himself inside me.

"Fuck," he moans into my neck, still squeezing me against him keeping us as close as possible while he rides out his orgasm.

We lay back on my bed, and I can feel his chest heaving beneath my own. "So, want to come over during lunch again tomorrow?" I ask playfully.

He kisses the top of my head and laughs. "I would come over every day just to see you come like that." Christ, he was making me eager to go again, and I'm still coming down from the first two orgasms.

Taking in the look on my face and where my mind is headed, he brings me back to focus. "It's a date. Which, speaking of, I feel like I owe you a proper first date." It's weird to think of how long we've known each other, and how we've already explored each other's bodies in so many ways, but we haven't had a first date.

"Oh yeah, what are you thinking?" I slide a leg up to his waist feeling him twitch beneath me. It's fun seeing the reactions I can get out of him.

Noah sits up on the bed and just smiles at me. "It's a surprise."

Great, now I have to sit around wondering what he was planning not knowing when it would happen. His schedule is so random, there's no set days he's on duty or off. Hell, it's been two weeks since the wedding already, and I've only seen him here twice, the first time being the night of my embarrassing nightmare. Which we still haven't talked about. It's almost like the longer we put it off, the harder it is to bring up. I know we're both aware of the situation and that we need to discuss things. But I'm enjoying this little bubble we've been in. It's blissful and easy right now. I don't want to be the reason that it gets messed up.

"I'm on duty in about an hour so I should probably get going. I'm sorry I made it look like I only came over for sex. That seriously wasn't my intention...though I don't regret it." He winks at me, and I can't help but smile. Everything about him has always made me melt in a way no one else can.

"Please. Come over anytime and distract me from my work. I was starting to go a little stir crazy when your perfect body and skilled tongue gave me just the release I needed."

I swing a leg over him so I'm straddling him, and instantly I'm wet again. I feel him twitch beneath me, fighting with himself. I know he has to get ready for work, and I still have lots to do myself. But two can play the torture game. "Are you sure you have to go?" I ask as I grind my hips against him feeling his thick erection slide between my folds again. I'm desperate to reenact what we just did not ten minutes ago.

Noah grips the back of my neck pulling my face to meet his. "You're playing with fire here, Eden. You know I'll flip you over and take you hard and fast right here, right now." He bites my earlobe, and I whimper against him.

"Oh, is that so?" I tease. "Let's see it," I challenge, calling his bluff and expecting him to take his leave like he said.

In one swift movement, so fast it's a blur, I'm face down on my bed with my ass in the air. Noah flipped me and grabbed my hips before thrusting into me so fast and hard I claw at the bedsheets as I cry out.

"You want to tease me like that? Let's see how well you take my cock when I'm slamming into you over and over again." He makes his point by pushing into me and stretching me as far as I can go. "You're so tight and ready for me. I can't get enough of you, Eden. Your pussy, your taste. Everything about you drives me wild." He's thrusting into me hard and fast, and it takes everything in me not to scream his name so loudly the walls shake.

How will I ever get enough of him? I want him all the time. Hell, I have him right now and still I want more. *"More."* I moan loudly, grinding my ass against him needing to feel another climax. The feel of him sheathing himself inside me is euphoric. I can feel every vein and sculpted muscle on him branding me from the inside out. He lowers his chest to lay across my back as he blazes a trail of kisses down my spine. He nibbles my flesh, and each time his tongue laps over a bite mark, it feels like he's branding my body. Ensuring that no inch of my skin goes untouched. He owns every part of my body, inside and out, etching himself on me like a tattoo.

We come together, and all I can hear is Noah's heavy breathing behind me and a ringing in my ears. Probably from how loud I was screaming his name. This time Noah really does need to go. We didn't intend to spend another thirty minutes wrapped up in each other, but the look on his face when he kisses me at the door says he'll take the punishment for being late. Now I'll be counting down the days until we can do that again.

32

Now

I turned in my article this morning, and as I walk toward the café, an overwhelming sense of ease comes over me. The air is cool and crisp, just enough of a chill to enjoy a sweater but not so cold my nipples cut slits in my shirt.

The bell above the door chimes as I walk through, and Jules waves to me. I smile in return and make my way to the counter.

"Jules, wait. I want to try something new today."

I gauge the look on her face to see if she's going to burst out laughing and make my regular anyway, or if she's malfunctioning from my abrupt changeup.

"Before you freak out, I want to stay in the same lane, just try something a little different. I trust you completely, so come up with something new." She's still staring at me, likely assessing if *I'm* the one malfunctioning before reluctantly nodding her head and getting to work.

"I warned you about this, you know?" she says from over the espresso machine. "I told you it would freak me out if you ever came in here asking for something new. Did something happen?"

"I'm just happy today. I don't know how to explain it," I tell her with a shrug.

"Okay. So, you want to make yourself unhappy by changing the drink you love? That makes total sense." Her words are dripping with sarcasm, and I can't help but smile.

"I'll love whatever you make, Jules. You're the best barista I know." Flattery gets her every time. She loves a good compliment.

"Okay, you weirdo, here you go." She smiles and hands over a hot white mocha latte with cold foam and caramel drizzle on top. I give her a look and take a small sip. I literally feel my eyes bug out and stare up at her with an unreadable expression.

"Shit, Jules." I'm still gaping at her, unable to say anything else.

"That bad or that good? You're making a weird face, so I really can't tell."

"That good. Jules, what the hell? I could have been trying other things this whole time instead of just sticking with what I know. I feel so dumb." To prove my point, I slap my hand across my forehead.

"Why are you slapping your forehead?" Chloe ambles up behind me looking more put together than I ever have been, rocking her heeled boots with black dress pants and the most amazing camel-colored pea coat. I'm going to try to steal that from her when she isn't looking.

"She just tried something new!" Jules yells from over the counter.

I roll my eyes and wait for the rant that's sure to come out of Chloe's mouth. I look up to find her staring at me, presumably with the same bug-eyed look I just gave Jules not five minutes ago. "You...you tried something different?" She shakes out her hand and lifts it to pretend to check my temperature.

"Quit it! Now who's the weirdo?" I laugh as I swat her hand away.

"Still you, Eden. Still you. Well? What did you get?" I fill her in on the heavenly goodness in a cup and offered her a taste before she asked Jules to make her the same.

"So, how are things with Noah? Are you ready to spill some details?" She props her face in one hand and gives me that innocent doe-eyed look. As if she's capable of looking innocent. When we were growing up, Chloe could never get away with anything. Her face always gave her away. It's like she didn't know how to pair certain situations with the right facial expression. It always made me laugh because without even defending herself with one word, her parents already knew it was a load of shit.

"Things are good, really good. But I'm not about to kiss and tell, Chlo." "That's such a stupid phrase, and you know it. I'm your best friend, and I've been dying to know how Noah is in the bedroom. It's been months since I've had a good lay, She tries her hand at puppy eyes, and all I can do is laugh.

Chloe is pouting as I check my text messages hoping for one from Noah. The espresso machine sputters behind me and the delicious smell of fresh coffee brewing is wafting all around us. Outside the leaves are blowing lightly, and it's almost like I can feel the cool air chilling my cheeks. No texts from Noah, which I shouldn't be surprised or disappointed by considering he's working. I just miss him; it's been five days since our little afternoon delight. It's all I've been able to think about.

"Earth to Eden," Chloe says while waving a hand back and forth in front of my face. "Where did you go just now?" she asks.

"Sorry, I zoned out for a minute."

"Thinking about that hot piece of man, no doubt." She licks her lips to emphasize her point, and I swat at her with my napkin.

Chloe's head is often in the gutter, but mine is, too, though, which is one of the many reasons we've always gotten along so well.

"Can you blame me? Everything about him screams *sex*." I bite my lip, remembering all the way we've been tangled up in each other.

"Which if you must know, is really, *really*, good. Like *amazing*." Now it's my turn to emphasize a little and maybe make her jealous.

"Ugh, I knew it. I can only imagine what those big hands can do..."

"Chloe, quit it! This is not something you can fantasize about right in front of me, and for that, you're officially weirder."

We laugh together and talk idly about mundane work stuff before she heads back to the office.

Since my article got turned in, I have the rest of the day to do what I want. I walk home slowly, peering into shops I never seem to have time to actually shop in. I talk for a few minutes with a nice older woman, Martha, about adding more Little Free Libraries around town and maybe even running a story about it. Hoping to influence the young minds of our town, she claimed.

I pass the pond and watch as the leaves fall softly into the water, noticing how much more the foliage has changed since I was last here. I really want to come back with Noah, but with his work schedule and my article, we haven't had the time. Only the few stolen moments that we spend mostly naked. I pull out my phone and shoot off a text to Noah.

> **Eden: Hey, are you free tonight?**

He texts back almost immediately.

> **Noah: Just got off actually. Heading home to shower then I'm all yours. Ideas?**

> **Eden: Meet me at my place in thirty?**

> **Noah: See you soon, beautiful.**

I walk the last few blocks home thinking about tonight. It's time we really talk about what happened, and I know exactly where I want to do it.

"God, you smell good," Noah mumbles into the dip of my neck, inhaling my scent.

We spent the first ten minutes after he got here tangled in each other's arms, kissing like two horny teenagers. His eyes locked onto mine with a gaze so intense, so hot, I might ignite from the inside out. But I needed to focus. Tonight, we were finally going to talk about everything. It's long overdue, and truthfully, I feel like we both need it.

"I was thinking we could go for a walk." I smile softly, feeling my nerves kick in. I don't want to do this, but I have to do this. If not for me, for the future we could build together. I don't want to start a serious relationship with secrets between us.

"Yeah, let's do it."

I reach for my jacket and bag, locking the door behind me as we head out into the cold air. It's chillier now that the sun has gone down, but it's comfortable still. I'm already sweating through my sweater at the thought of this conversation, so it's probably best we're outside anyway. I'm going to need the fresh air.

I guide Noah down Lydon toward the pond. His step falters slightly when he sees where we are, but he smiles at me reassuringly. "I haven't been here since that night we watched Pleasantville," he says softly.

"Truthfully, it took me some time before I could come back," I confess. "But now I love coming here to sit and just be. It's peaceful." Noah smiles at me again, and I get the sense he can feel what's coming. He knows it's time to get everything out in the open. I just hope he can be honest with me.

"I know you have questions, Eden, and things you want answers to. I've wanted nothing more than to explain my side of everything, but I just couldn't." We take a seat on our bench, the one we sat on that night over a decade ago. I can feel my nervous shakes already racking my body, and I try to shake it off.

Noah continues talking but looks at his entwined hands instead of at me. "Looking back on everything as an adult now, I feel so stupid. My logic was so far off from what's right, and honestly, I went through a phase where I was pissed at my parents for not telling me to man up. I should have been there for you, and I wasn't. It's something that has eaten me alive every day for ten fucking years. I hated thinking about you lying in that hospital bed wondering why I wasn't there. I knew it was hurting you, but I couldn't see you like that. Not after watching the accident and the aftermath unfold right in front of me. I was wrecked over it for so long I stopped counting." He pauses to take a breath, and as much as I want to interject, I get the feeling he needs to get everything off his chest.

"I was the reason you broke your ribs, Eden. The rational side of me knows that it wasn't my fault the bus flipped, but if I had been sitting in your seat, I wouldn't have landed on you, crushing you." Those last words come out in a whisper, like it's physically painful for him to relive those moments. I remember it all too well. The smell of the fire and dripping gasoline. The sounds of other students screaming and crying for help, while I just laid there wanting to sleep. I know I had a concussion after, but during the whole thing, I didn't feel much. It was after everything that the pain came.

"When I managed to get you off the bus, your body was just limp. I kept screaming your name to wake you, but you didn't. I started to panic, thinking I'd lost you. Thinking how there was *no way* I could lose you. Not after finally getting a piece of you. The thought that I was even a part of you getting hurt and potentially los—" He stops abruptly, unable to finish the words. I reach over and take one of his hands in mine. Giving him any kind of encouragement to continue, knowing he needs it. Hell, I need it right now, too.

I've spent years wanting to see this accident from Noah's eyes, and now that I am, it hurts. I hurt for him. I hurt at the memory of my injuries, how they could have been even worse. I hurt knowing that Noah felt, even for a short time, that he could have lost me or that he was in any way part of the reason I was hurt.

"Noah, look at me. I know you've heard these words from doctors and your parents, probably even my parents. But there was nothing you could have done to change that accident. You are not the reason I got hurt. You are the reason I *survived*."

He meets my gaze on that last word, letting it sink in for everything it is. I don't think he was ever told it from that point of view. He was likely always told that it wasn't his fault, that he couldn't have known.

"If you hadn't been there next to me that day, I wouldn't have made it off the bus. Everyone else around us was in a blind panic trying to get themselves off the bus, not worrying about anyone else. We were all so young, and that's what our parents ingrained into us from an early age. To take care of ourselves. I survived that day because of *you*." I can feel the tension in Noah's entire body, just radiating stress in waves. I don't want to make him feel worse about something so shitty that happened years ago, but I need him to understand why I was hurt and why I went off on him that night at the bar.

"You were everything to me, Noah. My best friend, and for so long, I wondered what I had done wrong to make you abandon me like that when I needed you the most. The night I saw you at the bar, I said some things…" I pause, trying to find the right way to explain myself.

"Everything I said was true, but I didn't mean to attack you in that way. I could have been calmer and given you a chance to explain your side. But I was so angry still. I just wanted you to hurt the way I had been hurt. When you sold the house and moved, I had to watch you leave, and it felt like you never even cared. That's what hurt the most, knowing we had this epic friendship, and you dropped it all without flinching."

I finish my rant, and we sit in silence for a few minutes. Listening to the bugs calling out around the pond, watching the fireflies dance around each other, and just enjoying the calm. I'm still gripping Noah's hand in mine, afraid if I let it go, he'll bolt. He squeezes it tightly and then pulls away to stand. Shit, he really is about to bolt. I wouldn't even know what to do if he walked away right now. I was able to let him go all those years ago, but now after having so much more of him…I don't think I could let go if I tried.

"Eden."

That's it, he just says my name, staring out over the pond while I wait for more.

"For so long, I felt like I was the reason you got hurt that day. I never once looked at it the way you just said, and I hate my fourteen-year-old self for not going to you in the hospital and every day after. Knowing you, you would have said those exact words back then, and we could have avoided all this shit. Everything that has kept us separated for ten fucking years. You needed me, and I wasn't there. For that, I will always be sorry. I'll do whatever I can to make it up to you for as long as you will have me. I just figured if I wasn't around to hurt you, you'd be better off."

He scuffs his foot in the dirt before taking the seat next to me again. He turns his entire body to face me, takes both of my hands in his and looks at me with a newfound peace. Something I didn't realize was missing until seeing it clearly on his face now.

"You are my everything, Eden. I've spent so many years just walking around looking for something that I could never find. *You.*" He gently holds my face between his hands and kisses me softly. I angle my head, needing more of him, and lean into the kiss, giving it all I have. This feels like our first real kiss since the one we had when we were fourteen. My body is on fire, feeling truly awake for the first time in who knows how long. I crawl into his lap, and we kiss for a while. Long enough that my butt is cold, and all I want to do is go home with Noah.

He pulls away from the kiss, leaving my eyes heavy and my body yearning for more. He places a kiss on my nose and regains my attention. "That night, at the bar. You told me you drove to my house and saw me with a brunette outside the house."

It's a statement, not a question, and I'm mortified he remembers that part. I yelled so many things at him I didn't expect him to recall it all. "I just wanted you to know her name is Bree." I hold my breath, because dammit I don't really want to hear about an ex right now. He can sense my thoughts and nudges my chin with his hand, so I look at his piercing green eyes.

"She was someone I met who was always going to the academy. We're actually still friends, and I think you would really like her..." Ha, as if, I want to say but keep my composure until he's finished. "And her girlfriend, Alex." She's gay? Well, shit. Now I really feel dumb.

I look at him with a stupid look on my face surely. Then he starts laughing. He is actually belly laughing at me right now, and I want to throat punch him. I'm about to tell him off when he kisses me hard and eagerly. "Baby, I am not laughing at you, I promise. But the look you just had on your face was the cutest thing I've ever seen, and now I want to find more ways to make you do it."

"Ha ha, very funny." I swat him on the arm, which does nothing to him because he's built like a Greek god. "I am mortified you even remember me saying that to you that nigh and even more humiliated I went to your house in the first place. I went with every intention of telling you off. Probably would have been a lot like that night four years ago, actually." We both laugh and even though everything still hurts, it's a different kind of hurt. It's the kind that I'm healed from and don't feel everyday anymore, but the kind that will always be a part of me. I will always remember what it felt like to watch him leave, to feel rejected.

Hearing his side now, and him hearing mine, opens up a part of me that feels hopeful. This was the barrier between us all these years. It's time we really go for it. Give this relationship a chance after years of disconnect. Even after all this time, he still understands me in a way no one ever has.

My teeth start chattering, and it's evident we should head home and warm up. Winter is fast approaching, but I feel nothing in my heart but warmth. "Let's get you home and warmed up," Noah says as he wraps his arm around me. "I plan on stripping you naked as soon as we walk through the door."

33

Now

'm done living in the past. I spent so many years torturing myself over what happened instead of moving on. Hearing Noah's side of everything helped ease my mind in a way I didn't expect. For so long, I assumed he left because he wasn't interested or just didn't care. I should have given him more credit than that, but at a young age, I didn't know what else to think.

As an adult it's easier to reason through things, accept them for what they are. At fourteen, I had only just begun exploring what it meant to like Noah. I hadn't ever felt in love or really knew what love was outside of my family, which is completely different. Truly the only thing that makes me sad is knowing we could have had more time together. We're making up for it now, but we still missed so much of each other's lives.

I didn't get to see him graduate from the academy or start his career as a police officer. We didn't know each other through college or see each other graduate. There's so much I still want to learn about him and the person he is now as an adult. Things between us have been good, like *really* good. But if I'm being honest with myself, sometimes I'm afraid to be happy.

If I let it all in, it might someday be gone. I know what it feels like to think you're losing everything you have, the *person* you need. Everything you love. I remember that feeling of not mattering to Noah, wondering if he'd come home. Fearing that it was really over and that he wanted to leave me, and then he did. So now, even when things are good, I'm afraid to fully let myself be happy. I can still feel my walls slightly up, and all I want to do is lower them and give everything I have to Noah. Sometimes I tell myself he's halfway out the door so it won't hurt as much if he actually leaves again.

When the doubt creeps in, I often remind myself that when you go through a change in life, it's best to focus on what you're gaining rather than what you're losing. I may have lost Noah for a while, but we've found each other again, and all I want to do is move forward. I love him. I have *always* loved him. Instead of hiding that feeling away deep inside, I can let it out and enjoy it…finally.

If I'm lucky, I get Noah at least once or twice a week. His schedule changes often so I take what I can get. I never thought I would be dating someone who puts their life on the line every single day, and I'd be lying if I said it didn't scare me. A man in uniform is seriously sexy, but when responsibility and obligation is tied to that uniform, it makes it hard to always just fantasize. Halloween is approaching, and I want to ask Noah to wear his costume, just for me. I've never been one for role play, but I could be into it now that I have a cop boyfriend.

We have never had an official girlfriend/boyfriend conversation, but it was strongly implied after sleeping together. Being with Noah is like having all my teenage fantasies come to life. In high school, even when we weren't talking, he was so good looking it almost hurt to look at him. I wouldn't let myself pine over someone who didn't even want me, but I definitely checked him out. It all feels so silly now, knowing he liked me, and I liked him, but that we couldn't just talk and figure our shit out.

Noah is coming over tonight, and all I can think about is my need for him. The ache between my legs is almost too much to bear just thinking about how he makes me feel. I blush thinking about the night he stayed over last week. As soon as he walked through the door, I could feel my need coiling for him as he sauntered toward me. He pushes me up against the wall and drives his hardness right where I need him.

"Do you see what you do to me, Eden? I've only just walked in the door, and already I can smell how much you want me." He runs his nose up the inside of my neck until he meets my ear. "You are delectable, and if you'll let me, I plan on eating you alive tonight."

My knees shake as he speaks, knowing just what his tongue and expert fingers are capable of. I've never felt so desired, so craved, in my whole life. Sure, I'd been with other guys, but it was never anything like it is with Noah. He worships my body, touching me in all the right places. Taking me to the highest highs and caressing me as I come down just before doing it all over again. Noah is an addiction, something I should be embarrassed by, but oddly am excited by.

He strips off my shirt, baring my lace bra, and his eyes go dark. This is his favorite, the one I wore the night we first spent together after the wedding.

"Did you wear that just for me, baby?" I nod my head and bite my lower lip. "As much as I love it on you, I want to rip it from your body and feast on your chest." He unhooks it at the same time he says that, and my vision blurs. Noah looks absolutely hungry for me, and the feeling is empowering. I love knowing that I take him to this place, where he can lose himself in me, and me in him.

Using both hands, he lifts me under my thighs and wraps me

around his waist, just to lean in and suck one of my waiting nipples into his hot mouth. I arch into him and grind against his length, trying to find some release. A breathy moan escapes me, and the sound turns Noah frantic. He's guiding me toward the chair in the corner sitting in front of my desk, lowering himself onto it. I straddle him as I work the buttons free on his shirt. The feel of his chest beneath my fingertips is heavenly, and I lean in to lick all the way up his firm abs. His muscles ripple beneath my light touch, and I know I'm driving him mad.

I lift up to pull my shorts to the side, exposing myself to him. He takes in the fact that I'm not wearing any underwear and captures my mouth with his in a rough kiss. He swallows my gasps as I grind against him harder, needing to remove all the barriers between us. I undo his belt and unzip his jeans before sliding them down as best I can from my position. I place him at my entrance and slowly sink down onto him, reveling in the feel of him. His hard length starts pumping into me with such force my chest is shaking and heaving right in front of Noah's face. He steals a nipple between his teeth while twisting the other with his fingers. I cry out and claw against his bare back muscles.

I'm grinding into him like my life depends on it, seeking out that high only Noah can bring me to. I'm so close when Noah reaches around and grips my backside pulling me impossibly closer to him. The pressure is building, and I feel myself losing control, needing to give myself over to the sensations. I flush my chest against his and arch against him so I can feel the pressure on my clit. As soon as I start rotating my hips against him, I'm lost. Spiraling into oblivion, riding out the waves as they keep coming and coming. Noah's name is the only thing falling from my lips.

I draw in ragged breaths as I come down from the high Noah just brought me to. I know the risk of letting him back in, all the way in. The first time nearly tore me apart. I can't keep holding onto the fear it'll happen again. Caught up in the moment of euphoria, I grip Noah's neck, dragging his lips to mine before saying, "I love you." The admission catches us both off guard, and I blush a deep scarlet realizing that wasn't in my head.

"That wasn't...I didn't mean to say..." I can't find the right words to explain why I just said that. I'm hoping he'll save me from myself, but he's just looking at me, waiting for me to continue. "I'm sorry, I didn't mean to just spring that on you like that. I was lost in the moment, and it just slipped. But...it's not a lie. I—I do love you, Noah. I always have." I'm looking down at my hands clasped at the base of Noah's stomach, feeling more embarrassed than ever. He grips my chin and lifts my gaze to his.

"It's about time, Eden." He chuckles and kisses me with a softness. Now I'm the one just looking at him waiting to understand what he means. "I've loved you my whole life. I left because I loved you, and I came back because I love you. There's no one else out there for me. Just you." My eyes are glassy, and I can feel tears threatening to fall, but Noah starts moving in me again slowly. His eyes are locked on mine, and I couldn't look away if I tried. We are connected physically and emotionally, all parts of me, inside and out, are a part of Noah. My heart beats for him and always has.

He continues his pace, moving a little quicker now and holds me as we climax together. Finally releasing years of unspoken love for one another. This was worth the wait.

***

I'm brought out of my memories when my phone rings next to me. No one calls me anymore, except my mom. Usually, my friends just text me. I don't recognize the number, so I send it to voicemail and place my phone on the coffee table. Noah is coming over in a few hours so I might as well clean up my apartment and make it look nice so we can destroy every surface later on.

Two hours later all the dishes are done, dried and put away. Laundry is folded and in its rightful place. Clean sheets are on my made-up bed, and candles light the area with a soft glow. The scent of brownies fills the space around my apartment mixing with the garlic I'm chopping for dinner. We decided to stay in tonight, watch Pleasantville, since I haven't been able to watch it again since that night, and have a home cooked meal. I'm not a bad cook, but fettuccine alfredo is my specialty. A fresh salad, garlic bread, and wine tops off the whole package. All that's left is to wait for Noah to get here.

We agreed on seven tonight since he was supposed to be off duty around five. He had said he wanted to get in a gym session with Remi then head home to shower. It's now seven thirty, and though it's only been half an hour, I'm starting to worry. It's not like him to be late, and if he was running late, he would have texted me. I check my phone when I realize it's been sitting on the coffee table for the last couple hours, knowing he probably texted me. I feel silly getting myself worked up, but sometimes I get a bad feeling when I don't hear from him.

I sigh in relief when I see a missed call and voicemail. He probably called on his way over here. I check the time and see the call came in over two hours ago. The unknown number I sent to voicemail. A wave of unease settles over me as my fingers hover, trembling, over the one voicemail. I hit play, and Michelle's frantic voice sounds through the speaker. She got my number from my mom apparently. I can hardly understand her. She's talking a million miles a second, and I'm trying to decipher what she's saying when all I catch is *"Noah'* and *"hospital'*. The phone falls from my hand and clatters to the floor. I can't move, can't breathe, can't process. This can't be real.

34

Now

The parking lot of the hospital is packed. It creates an uneasy feeling in my chest knowing that many people are potentially injured or sick there. Loved ones could be receiving bad news as we speak, and I'm sitting here in my car being a coward. I'm afraid to walk in there and see Noah hurt. I can't imagine his perfect face, strong arms, and amazing smile being anything but. The last few weeks have been almost too good to be true. Since we had the talk at the pond, we've moved forward and just focused on getting to know each other again. I'm not ready to lose him again.

Another forty-five minutes later, and I'm still in the exact same spot. My hand is hovering by the door handle, and I desperately want to go in. But there's something holding me back, and I can't place it. I haven't been back in this hospital in ten years, not since my accident. It was inside that building I realized Noah wasn't coming to see me, that things were different. A tear slides down my face, and I just want to scream into the night sky.

I release my anger on my steering wheel while I cry like a lunatic. I hope no one is nearby, or they might think I escaped the psych ward. I know I need to be there for him, hold his hand and comfort him, even if he isn't awake to see me. I *want* to be there for him, and that feeling just reminds me that he didn't *want* to be there for me all those years ago.

I'm seeing everything in a different light now. He wanted to be there, he just *couldn't*. My mind is reeling, and my breathing is ragged as I come to terms with the fact that Noah wanted to be here. He wanted to protect me, keep me safe, and have me as his. But he didn't think he was worthy of any of it. He was too afraid to face me, and I spent years being crushed by his absence. Here I am faced with a similar situation, and I can't open the fucking car door. I'm a hypocrite.

I can honestly say I am wholeheartedly in love with this man. I have been my whole life. The only feeling that can ever overcome love is fear. I fear he isn't going to make it, and I cannot walk in there just yet and be smacked with that reality.

Turning the key in the ignition, I put the car in reverse and slowly back out. I cry the whole way home and even more as I sit on my couch, wrapped in blankets, crying into a gallon of ice cream. A part of me wants to call the girls and beg them to sit with me, coddle the coward as her boyfriend lies injured in a hospital bed wondering where I am. As appealing as that comfort sounds right now, I know I need to be alone. Prepare myself for the worst case scenario while simultaneously hoping for the best.

I debate calling Michelle so she can fill me in on his injuries, but that would require me admitting I didn't go to him. Not exactly a conversation I'm prepared to have. Though she's an understanding woman, I imagine she would have some feelings about her son's girlfriend not being by his side. He may have done the same to me, but we were fourteen, and that was a long time ago. Plus, two wrongs don't make a right. I can practically hear those words falling from my mom's mouth. Her voice comes over my thoughts and reminds me once again I'm not doing my part here. When a person you love and care for is hurt, you're supposed to be there for them.

My phone screen is cracked from when I dropped it on the floor after getting the news. I pick it up and dial my mom's number while biting my nails nervously. She answers on the second ring. "Oh Eden, how is he honey? Michelle called a little while ago and said she told you. I've been wanting to call but figured I'd wait to hear from you." She rushes out the words quickly, probably half expecting me to break out in tears.

"Well, that's kind of while I'm calling," I pause trying to catch my breath after crying for so long. My mouth is dry, and my throat is sore. "I haven't gone to see him yet. I mean, I tried, but I couldn't get out of the car." She's quiet on the other end of the line, likely thinking about her response.

"I think that's perfectly understandable, sweetie."

As much as it helps that my mom isn't making me feel bad for staying away, I wasn't at all expecting her to understand. "You do?" I ask hesitantly.

"Of course. You guys just got to know each other again. I can't imagine you were prepared for something like this to happen so soon into your rekindling. That's a lot for anyone, especially given the history between you two." Mom is so intentional with her words; she thinks things through and has an appropriate response to everything. Note to self—be more like that.

"I spent so many years upset with him for not being by my side, and here I am doing the same thing. It's not right, I know it's not, but I just can't, Mom." I start to cry again, unable to control the flow of tears. One would think I'd have nothing left after how much crying I've already done.

The sound of keys jingling in the background and a door opening catches my attention through the tears. "Are you going somewhere?" I ask her through my sobs.

"Oh, just to the store quickly. I'm still here honey, as long as you need me." She stays on the phone with me for another fifteen minutes until my tears have slowed down and my breathing is less choppy. I assure her I'm okay and hang up the phone.

Not even a minute later, there's a knock on my door. I'm sure I look wrecked, but at this point I don't even care. I trudge over to the door wrapped in a fluffy blanket while my slippers shuffle across the floor. Standing in the doorway with a bunch of treats and a bottle of wine is my mom. I burst into tears again and fall into her arms. Even as an adult, I still need my mom. Whenever I need her, she's there.

Dropping the canvas bags on the counter, she pulls me in with both arms and holds me tight for several minutes while I cry whatever is left in me onto her shoulder. "I can't believe you came over here," I sniffle against her.

"I don't care if I'm only down the road or a thousand miles away. If my baby needs me, then I'm here." Guiding me over to the couch, she plops me back into my cocoon of blankets and heads to the cabinets for some wineglasses. I don't question her when she pulls three from the shelf. I just bury my face into more tissues.

Finding a tray in the closet, she loads it up and brings it to the coffee table overflowing with all my favorites. A mountain of Twix bars, brownies from the bakery down the street, popcorn, and of course, my favorite Riesling. Taking a much-needed sip, I look down into my glass and swirl the clear liquid around. Mom places her hand on my knee and gives it a gentle squeeze. "How about some TV?" she says as she reaches for the remote. I snuggle against her propping my head on her shoulder as she starts up season one of *Gilmore Girls*. Mom always watched this show with Callie and me, saying we had a similar relationship as Lorelei and Rory. She probably hasn't seen it much since we both moved out, so her putting it on right now is exactly what I need.

Halfway through episode three, there's another knock at the door. Before I can sit up to answer, Mom just pats my knee as if telling me to stay put. The door opens, and Callie walks in looking winded like she ran here.

"Callie, what are you doing here?" My internal voice is excited and surprised to see her, but to her, it probably sounded strangled.

"Mom called me. I got in the car the second we hung up." She walks over to take the space on my right and wraps an arm around me. For what feels like the thousandth time tonight, I cry helplessly.

The three of us eat snacks, Lorelei and Rory style, and scarf down a large pizza. We finished the first bottle of wine and are well into our second. I'm still devastated by what happened to Noah, not that I have any details yet. I don't even know if his injuries are life-threatening. But with my mom and sister here, I can at least breathe a little easier. I'm not alone in dealing with my feelings. I'm with two people who understand me more than anyone. With their help, I know tomorrow I can make it to the hospital. I have to be there for him. More than anything else, I *want* to be there for him.

35

NOW

Last night was exactly what I needed. I didn't even realize how much I missed my mom and sister until they were here. I allowed myself a night to wallow, but now it's time to put on my big girl pants.

The phone rings three times before Michelle answers. "Good morning, Eden. What can I do for you?" She sounds normal, calm. That helps my nerves a little because if something was life-threatening with Noah, she'd be a mess.

"I'm headed to the hospital soon and wanted to see if there was anything I could grab for Noah." I don't even realize I'm pacing until I bump into the end table by the couch.

"That's lovely of you to offer, dear. Maybe you could stop by his place and grab some essentials? I'll text you a list." I smile, feeling more useful than I have in two days. The thought of seeing him in a hospital bed still makes me nauseous, but I feel stronger today. I can do this.

Thirty minutes later I'm unlocking the door to Noah's apartment. He had a key made for me not long after we started officially dating. He said he didn't want me to ever have to wait in the hall in case he was running late. He later admitted he wanted me to have the key so I felt I belonged here. Knowing how much he wanted me here gave me butterflies like a damn schoolgirl.

His apartment is very minimalist and clean, something you don't see from a lot of grown men. During one of our late-night talks once he told me being a police officer basically guarantees you messes every day. He wanted to come home to something serene and well-kept. Closing the door, I step into the apartment, taking in the space and wishing he were here, too. I've never been here by myself. It feels weird, like something is missing. Someone *is* missing, my inner monologue makes a snide comment at me. Ignoring her, I make my way to his bedroom to grab some things.

His walls are a light gray with a darker gray accent wall where his bed is made up. In his closet, I find a duffel bag and start filling it with comfortable clothes and his own pillow. Hospital gear is always so stiff and smells sterile. In his bathroom, I begin filling his toiletry bag, grabbing his toothbrush and deodorant from the side of the his-and-hers sink. In his dresser, I open the top drawer looking for boxers when something catches my eye. I know it's wrong to snoop, but who keeps one random envelope in the top drawer with their socks and underwear?

I'm about to close the drawer when my better judgment goes out the window, and I reach for the sealed envelope. Maybe it's a love letter from an old girlfriend he couldn't throw out, or some important document he wanted to keep safe in his top drawer, though, I thought that's what safes were for. I turn it over in my hands and gasp when I see my name scrawled across the front in Noah's handwriting.

The envelope looks weathered, like it's been around for a while. The coloring has faded, and the ink looks dull. This is old. I'm trying to convince myself to just put it back where it belongs and finish gathering his stuff, but I can't. I need to know what was so important he wrote it down but never gave it to me.

Walking over to the bed, I put the duffel bag on the floor and take a seat. My hands are shaking as I try to delicately tear the envelope open without destroying it. Taking a deep breath, I pull a single folded sheet out and stare at it for several minutes, trying to muster the courage to see the words.

Dear Eden,

You'll probably never read this letter, because even if I find the courage to send it, I can't picture you reading. Can't say I wouldn't deserve that. I'll never be able to apologize enough for shutting you out. You deserved answers, hell you still deserve them, and I wasn't strong enough to give you them. Everything happened so fast, and I truly thought I lost you. In my panic-stricken mind, I decided that if I couldn't keep you safe, then I didn't deserve you. Guess I'm not the most logical person in the world.

But you always called me predictable, and what hurts the most is that you never saw any of this coming. For that, I am so sorry, Eden. You mean the absolute world to me, and if I was strong like you, I would have told you this in person.

We're moving tomorrow, and all I can think about is having one more movie night with you. A part of me feels like if I went over there right now, you'd let me in. We'd just go back to being Noah and Eden, but that would be selfish of me, and again, you deserve more than that.

The main thing I want to give you is some reassurance. None of this was your fault Eden, please believe that. It's not because I don't like you or don't want to be with you. Believe me when I say, that's all I think about. But almost losing you made me realize I can't be in a world where you don't exist.

One day I'll become a police officer, and maybe then I'll be worthy of you and can protect you. I love you, Eden. Every part of me is yours, and until I'm ready to give that to you, I hope you're happy. More than anything else, I want you to be happy.

Love, Noah

Tears are streaming down my face, a few drops landing on the page. I wipe them away before they have the chance to smear the writing. I keep rereading it, letting all his emotion seep into me. The day he moved, he kept looking up at my house, as if willing me to come outside. I wonder if I had, he would have given me the letter. Would I have just forgiven him and gone on the way we used to be? Knowing me, and my feelings for him, I likely would have. I just wish I'd known all of this back then. Things could have been so different. All this time he didn't think he deserved me, that I was worth more. Little did he know, I felt like I wasn't good enough, and that's why he left.

God, what a little communication could have done for us back then. I sigh into my hands, wiping the remnants of tears off my face. I gathered his things and the letter, ready to head to the hospital and see him. First, I need to stop back home and grab something of my own.

Walking into the hospital, I feel the anxiety I did yesterday sitting in my car. At least I made it into the building this time. I go to check in and grab a photo sticker before heading to the elevators. I hope no one else is here visiting right now, I doubt I'd be able to hold it together very long, and today doesn't feel like a good day to embarrass myself. I stop at the information desk to ask the nurse what room Noah Rivers is in. She points me in the right direction, and I make it to his door before panic really sets in.

I lean my body against the wall next to his door and allow myself several deep breaths before knocking lightly on the door. There's no answer, so that either means he's asleep, or that no one is in there. I'm hoping it's the latter. My hands are so clammy the door handle slips from my grip before I'm able to successfully open the door. "m immediately hit with beeping sounds from various machines. Everything smells sterile, and the furniture looks like something from the eighties and very uncomfortable. At least he has a nice view of the bay from his window, not that he's been sitting there gazing out at it, I'm sure. Luck would have it, no one else is in here right now. I don't think I would have been able to do this if there was company here to witness how nervous I am.

On the bed, Noah lies there motionless with his eyes closed. I don't want to wake him, so I take this quiet time to study his features, and all the cuts and scrapes on his face. It looks like a makeup kit blew up in his face. There are mottled bruises over his eyes and deep red cuts trailing down one cheek. I wish I could kiss every single injury until he felt better, but I would probably cause him more discomfort than help.

His chart is hanging by his bed, so I quietly grab it and try to understand what I can. A gasp slips free, and I right myself before Noah wakes up. Walking over to the chair in the corner, I take a seat and read his *list* of injuries. He was in a serious car crash during a chase. When the airbag deployed, it broke his nose, which explains the double black eyes. The cut down his cheek is from broken glass when the window broke. That has ten stitches. Oh God, I feel like I can't breathe. He suffered six broken ribs, a partially collapsed lung and a broken leg. Out of all the injuries listed here, the broken leg will piss him off the most. Knowing Noah, he's going to want to get up and go back to work right away.

Six to eight weeks of physical therapy, at least, for his leg, and a couple weeks for the bruising and cuts to fade. Despite everything, he's still as insanely gorgeous as always. I walk back to the side of his bed and sit in the chair taking his hand. I rub like circles over and over when suddenly one of his finger's flinches. "Noah?" I ask hesitantly, still unsure if he's sleeping.

"E-Eden? Are y-you really h-here?" He's stuttering and sounds exhausted, probably from the partially collapsed lung. I'd be winded, too, if I were him.

"I'm here, Noah. I'm sorry I wasn't here earlier, but I'm here now. Rest, baby. I'm not going anywhere." I kiss his temple and keep his hand in mine. We stay like that for another two hours before he starts to wake up. Seeing him open his eyes and smile has my heart catapulting in all different directions. Different scenarios are bouncing around my head causing panic to rise. It could have been so much worse, he could have been more seriously injured, or he could have…I can't even bring myself to think that last thought. All I can do is remind myself he's here, he's alive, and he *will* recover. If I know one thing is certain, it's that he will do everything in his power to be back on his feet as soon as possible.

"Hi, beautiful." His voice sounds like velvet caressing my skin in the most heavenly way. I never thought I could swoon over a voice, yet here I am. A tear starts to slide down my cheek, but I wipe it away quickly and try to smile. Noah can see through my bullshit and tries to calm me. He's the one who was in a serious car accident, lying in a hospital bed with a whole slew of injuries, and yet here he is trying to make *me* feel better.

"I'm so sorry. I really wanted to be strong." I laugh as I wipe away another tear. "You're the one hurt, and I'm crying like a baby."

He squeezes my hands and whispers for me to look at him. "I'm happy you're here. There's no one else I wanted to see more than you." His face falls slightly, dropping his gaze to our joined hands. "Eden, I just wan—"

He starts, but I cut him off. "Don't. I know what you're thinking, and a lot has changed, Noah. I know how you felt back then. I don't hold it against you. Okay?"

"But still, I know how much you wanted me there, and I wasn't, I mean I couldn't…I just wish I could have told you that back then."

Even though I'm embarrassed for snooping, I'm glad I brought his letter with me. "So, I have a confession to make. I hope you aren't mad, and it sure as hell wasn't premeditated. But I went to your place to grab some essentials for you, and well, I found this in your top drawer." I pull out the envelope, all evidence that it was ripped open apparent. I turn it over in my hands revealing my name scrawled across the front.

"I would never snoop through your things, but I saw my name, and something came over me. I knew it was wrong, but I couldn't help myself. I'm really sorry." I look down at the envelope, afraid to meet Noah's eyes, and take a deep breath before continuing.

"But I need you to know, your words were beautiful. I wish more than anything we could have just communicated with each other back then. I would have understood." He nods his head, listening to everything I've just confessed.

"That's the thing, Eden. I didn't want you to just understand and forgive me. The way I handled things was wrong. I knew it then, and I know it now. I wrote that letter to make myself feel better, knowing you weren't likely ever going to read it, to apologize in at least one way since I couldn't to your face. You deserved more than a boy who couldn't face you when things got tough."

"We both could have handled it differently. I could have gone to you and demanded answers, knowing you would have at least talked to me. But I shut you out, too, and never really looked at it like that because I was too upset." We're both crying now, unashamed of our emotions.

"The day I saw the '*for sale*' sign in front of your house, I was heartbroken. Lying in my bed, unable to accept that it was true, I channeled my emotions into anger instead of depression and jumped to my feet. I tore down every one of those stars you helped me hang when we were kids. The reminder of them above me every single night was too much. Having you still next door gave me hope, but seeing you leave felt like it was over." I'm ranting and breathing heavily, but I continue.

"I threw the stars in the trash and promised myself I was going to remove you from my life, like the stars on the ceiling." I glance up to see him looking at me meaningfully, as if he understands my reasoning back then.

"As easy as it was to just rip them down, it wasn't that easy to remove you from my mind. I knew a part of you would always be there, a part of me." I reach into my bag and pull out my diary, something I haven't looked at in years, covered in a layer of dust on top. I open it up and pull out the single star I saved.

"I saved one star, Noah. Just one to be that reminder I knew I would need one day. I've saved it all these years with the hope that maybe we could have one more chance. I could never remove you from my life completely. There was always this small piece of you with me." I carefully place the star in his palm and wait for some kind of reaction.

Noah is gazing at the star like it's a rare diamond I just placed in his hand. A few more tears roll down his cheek, mirroring the tears rolling down my own. "You are my star, Noah. I always wished for you." Wiping his eyes, he pulls on my hand, gesturing for me to come closer.

"Come here, I need to kiss you." I laugh weakly, still feeling the heaviness of this moment, but I lean in and gently brush my lips against his. "I guess we'll have to keep things a little mellow for the next few weeks." He winks, there's my Noah. I smile.

"Seriously, Eden." He holds my cheek and stares directly into my soul. I can feel my heart bursting more than I ever thought possible. My insides feel like lava heating me from the inside out. "You are my whole world, I revolve around you, like you are the sun. Which luck has it, happens to be a star." He smiles and holds up the little plastic star. "ve never felt more in love with someone than at this moment here. "There will always be dark moments in life, and when those dark moments emerge, that's when I see you. My little star." The tears flow freely now, and I lean down to kiss him again, a little more eagerly than before.

We get a few more minutes alone before the nurse comes in to administer more pain meds. Shortly after that, his parents and Charlie arrive. I slip out to get something to eat in the cafeteria, when I hear John, his dad coming up behind me. "Oh, hi, Mr. Rivers It's been a long time." I say awkwardly, not sure how to talk apparently.

"Eden, please, I've known you most of your life. Call me John." I nod my head in understanding.

"I'm just heading to the cafeteria, care to join me?" I ask, him not thinking he actually wants to.

"I'd love to."

On the elevator down, John clears his throat and speaks up. "Listen, I just want to get something off my chest." Oh crap, I knew there was a reason he agreed to come with me. I swallow the lump forming in my throat and squeak out a quiet *"okay""*

"Noah was wrong back then. He should have shown up for you, and he didn't. I'm sorry about that. Michelle and I like to think we raised our boys to be respectful and strong, and I believe since then, he has proven he is." I want to interject and tell him that he is, we've overcome so much since then. But I let him continue. "You being here for him, for standing by him. We...I am grateful, Eden. I know Michelle is, too, but I need you to hear from me how happy we are that you're back in his life."

This is the longest conversation I've ever had with Mr. Rivers. I was always a little intimidated by him as a kid. He has never been a man of many words. This here feels like a turning point, and all I can do is smile. Before the moment passes, I lean over and wrap him in a hug. I know it startled him initially, but soon the tension releases from his shoulders, and he hugs me back. The only thing going through my mind as we exit the elevator is family. That is what the Rivers family is to me.

36

NOW

It's been six weeks since the accident, and Noah is recovering well. His mom stayed with him the first week, and by the end of the seven days, I wasn't sure who was ready to strangle whom. Listening to them bicker always made me laugh, which usually annoyed them, only resulting in me laughing harder. We're on our way to physical therapy, and the doctors are all impressed with how quickly Noah is recovering, as am I. The sooner he recovers, the sooner we can get back to normal, something Noah is *really* anxious for.

Intimacy has been a lot harder since his accident, we need to be careful and take things slow, something very difficult for us both. Anytime I see him kicking ass in physical therapy shirtless, I want to rip the remaining clothes from his body and ravage him. This appointment will be our answer as to whether he's ready to fully return to regular activities, or if he needs to take it easy for a couple more weeks. The PT office is connected to the back of the hospital, so we park in the designated lot and walk in.

Shortly after, the doctor comes into the office with a smile. "Well, Noah, you certainly are impressive. If only all my patients were as dedicated as you." He plops into his chair and folds his hands on his desk. "You're clear. Your leg has healed beautifully, PT was a breeze for you, and the x-rays show no signs for concern. Congratulations, Officer Rivers."

Something about hearing that makes my heart swell. Noah was hurt on the job, protecting this city while putting his own life at risk. It's something I will never take for granted. I'm so proud of him, and judging by the look on his face, he's proud of him, too.

"Thank you, Dr. Litchfield. It's been a pleasure working with you here. I just want to clarify one thing before we go…" He's not about to ask him. 'e's smiling that smile of his. He's going to ask the one question I was hoping he wouldn't. Bracing myself, I put one hand over my face as Noah starts to speak. "When you say all clear, you mean we can resume…regular activities as well, right?" He didn't say it outright, but the implication is there, and I'm mortified. With a chuckle, Dr. Litchfield smiles, "Yes, you can resume having intercourse." Ugh, kill me now.

We stand and shake hands, my face and skin very noticeably on fire, and exit the office. "I cannot believe you asked that!" I swat his arm not even caring if I hurt him at this point. "You knew what he meant when he said, *'all clear'* and you asked anyway!"

My face is still beet red, and Noah takes it in his hands and smiles. "Of course, I knew. But what fun would that have been?" He kisses me playfully then tugs me to the car quickly.

"What's the rush, we don't have anywhere else to be right?" I ask him confused as he lifts me into the Jeep, strapping me in. "On the contrary, Ms. Walker. We indeed have somewhere very important we need to be." He hops in the driver's seat and starts backing out of the parking lot.

"I believe we have some catching up to do. Six weeks is a long time not to have you under me the way I want you, Eden." My skin is ablaze

with need, and the ache between my legs is almost too much to bear.
I wet my lips before responding. "Your place or mine?"

37

AGE 10

Noah and I are hiding out in our fort, the makeshift one we made in his basement that has held up for two weeks now. We built it so carefully so we could keep it. Now we just want to see how long it lasts before it falls apart. Michelle let us order a couple of pizzas for our movie night, extra cheese for me, pepperoni for Noah, and a bunch of snacks.

Being in the basement is almost like having your own place. No one ever really comes down here unless Michelle has laundry to do, so we have the place to ourselves. Noah and I stay up late, watching movies, eating junk food, and talking all night. I always wind up sleeping for hours the next day when I get home. Even when I'm exhausted, I push myself to stay up as late as possible, just like Noah. He always beats me, though.

Tonight, we're watching one of my picks, *Dirty Dancing*. Noah made a face at first, but I told him he had to watch with me since I watch his favorites with him. He agreed, and now I think he might actually be enjoying the movie. He'll never admit it, though, that I know. "Why does everyone call her *Baby*?" Noah asks with a mouthful of popcorn. I roll my eyes and throw a handful of mini Twix at him.

"They told you in the beginning, weren't you paying attention?" He just shrugs his shoulders and goes back to watching.

I love our movie nights. I hope we never stop having them, even when we're older. Pretty soon our parents aren't going to let us have sleepovers together anymore. Mom tried explaining it, but I didn't see the problem. She just said I would understand when I'm older, whatever that means. For now, I'll just enjoy it while we have it because Noah is my best friend in the whole world, and nothing will change that. I'm wrapped up in some of my softest blankets. I'm here so much that I left a few for when we have our sleepovers and look over at Noah. He's still stuffing popcorn into his mouth at an unhealthy speed and staring intently at the screen. It's the part when Baby and Johnny are practicing the lift part of their routine in the water, one of my favorite parts.

"Hey, Noah?" I nudge him until he's paying attention.

"What's up, E?" he responds, a few popcorn pieces falling out.

"Promise me we'll always be best friends?" I ask, holding out my pinky for him to take with his.

He looks at me and smiles, nodding his head, "Promise."

EPILOGUE

THREE YEARS LATER

"**H**urry up, or I'm going to start the movie without you, E!" Noah yells at me from our couch. *Our* couch. I just love the way that sounds. We moved in together about six months ago. Had it been up to Noah, we would have moved in together the day he got cleared for his leg. We went back to his place and devoured each other all night. By morning my body was deliciously sore, and I was happy. Elated, even. But for some reason that word always sounds cheesy. We ultimately decided to take our time. We had waited years to be together, and we didn't want to rush things just to mess them up.

So, six months ago we started looking for places together. After a week of debate and many horrible apartments later, we decided to buy a house. We'd been together over two years at that point and knew it was the best decision for us. Our moms thought we should get married first, but we wanted to do things our way.

"I'm coming. You're so impatient!" I snap back playfully from the kitchen. I walk through the wide archway between the dining room and the living room where Noah is cozy on the couch, remote in hand. "What movie did you decide on anyway? It's your pick tonight."

Pressing play, he leans over giving me a quick peck. "Oh, I know. You're going to love it." Why does it feel like he's tricking me, and I'm about to watch some gruesome horror film that will keep me from sleeping the next several days. Just then the opening for "Be My Baby" by The Ronettes starts playing, and my hand freezes midair with popcorn falling to my lap.

"It's still one of your favorites, right?" Noah asks, pulling me from my thoughts.

"Yeah…you remembered the night we watched it?" I ask, feeling tears prick my eyes for some reason.

"I do. We promised to be best friends forever that night." I nod my head, remembering it as if we pinky swore yesterday, down in Noah's basement safely wrapped up in our fort.

"Here's the thing. I don't want to be best friends anymore." I'm immediately taken back, trying to process what he means. We finally bought a house together; we've been dating for three years now, and we just adopted the cutest yellow lab puppy named Chowder. Is he that bored with me already?

Noah can see the panic painting my face and grabs my hand. "Eden, you are my best friend. You're my everything. I made a promise I intend to keep forever. But I'm thinking I'm ready to make another promise tonight. If you'll allow me, that is." The color is now draining from my face just as quickly as it recovered not ten seconds ago. Noah reaches across the coffee table and to pick a Twix bar.

"Twix bars were never my favorite. I always got them because of you. Even when we were estranged, I would buy a Twix bar every time I went to the store because it reminded me of you. Soon, they became my favorite, too." He opens the Twix bar and hands me the left side. "I've given a lot of thought to how I wanted to do this, from big gestures to here at home. This is a place we created together, a place where we love, fight sometimes, and build our future." Tears are falling down my face in waves at this point, and my hands are so clammy, I'm melting the chocolate bar.

"When we were ten years old, I promised to be your best friend forever, and I will hold true to my word. Can you promise me something in return?" he asks, and now is the first time I've heard the wavering in his voice. Just slightly, but I can hear the nerves. I stare at him wide-eyed and nod my head. "You're my sun, Eden. I revolve around you, and when the world gets dark, you're there to brighten it up. I can't change what happened in the past, but I can promise you something for our future."

He pulls out a stunning radiant-cut diamond, flanked by what looks to be almost thirty tiny diamonds circling the rest of the band. My eyes have bugged out of my skull at this point, barely breathing with tears soaking my T-shirt now.

"You are radiant in every way possible, hence the shape of the diamond. And these"—he points to all the diamonds, sparkling like tiny stars, all around the band—"these represent every year I've loved you. If you'll do me the greatest honor." He stands up from the couch and gets down on one knee, holding my left hand in his.

"Promise you'll be my wife and make me the happiest man in the world." I'm crying uncontrollably now with the biggest smile on my face. I nod my head up and down while Noah slides the ring onto my finger.

I kiss him slowly, passionately, and we fall to the floor in a heaping mess of limbs and blankets. Chowder barely notices and just grunts in his sleep. "It wasn't until I was faced with darkness that I saw you. Yes, a million times."

26

Age 21

Yesterday I found out I got accepted to my dream school, Columbia University, and today I'm in my fourth year here. How I managed to make it to my senior year in the blink of an eye is beyond me. But here we are. I stayed true to my plan and went with the undergraduate creative writing program, something I haven't regretted for a second. Sure, the work is hard, and I've had some strict professors, but I love it.

I still haven't decided if I want to go for my master's or not. I may take some time off and experience real-world work first. I can always go back for my master's in a few years. In the last few weeks, I've been researching what company I want to work for and building my resume. I've even considered starting my own blog, but with my classwork load, I tabled that idea.

Freshman year I met two girls who were on the same floor as me in the dorms—Stella and Emmy. We hit it off immediately and requested to room together the following year. We've been inseparable ever since. To make things even better, Chloe loves them as much as I do, so the four of us have become close. Tonight we're heading out to a bar in the city hoping to blow off some steam before finals and graduation.

Once we're all ready, we decide to walk to the bar, so no one has to be a designated navigator. We all went out one night and took the subway, which ended up being a huge mistake. We were too drunk to properly figure out how to get home, so we ended up an hour away from the dorms.

Blowfish is a cool bar we frequent regularly. The floors have teal blue tiles that glow like you're walking on water. The wall behind the bar is one huge fish tank with real fish swimming about. I've always wondered how they clean the thing without knocking over all the bottles lining the bar shelves. One of these days I'm just going to ask.

Making our way over to the bar, we flag down Shay, the bartender. She's one of the coolest people I've met since moving to the city. There are about five piercings on her face, along with dozens of tattoos covering most of her body. She has gorgeous long hair that's mostly a magenta color, and she is *always* wearing black. The last fact is what we bonded over initially. Truth be told, I was afraid to even talk to her because she seems like the type of girl who would hurt you with just one look. Turns out she's incredibly sweet and is a culinary student. We give her our drink orders and wait by the end of the bar, looking around at the growing crowd.

There's a group of really hot guys standing at one corner of the bar looking past the dance floor. I'm not one to hook up with random guys, but the stress of finals looming has me wanting to let loose. Something about one of the guys has goose bumps rising up my arms instantly. His back is to me so I can't see his face, but it's the way he's standing there, clearly engaged in conversation but shuffling his foot against the tiles.

I don't even realize Chloe has been trying to get my attention until she positions her body directly in front of me blocking my view and bringing me back to reality. "Eden, what's up? You look like you've seen a ghost," she asks. I try to look over her shoulder, convinced I'm